◄Baxie Randall

◄Randall

AND THE BLUE RAIDERS

GRIERSON'S RAID

APRIL 17

LAGRANGE

RIPLEY

NEW ALBANY

PONTOTOC

HOUSTON

CLEAR SPRING

STARKVILLE

COLUMBUS

LOUISVILLE

MACON

PHILADELPHIA

DECATUR

VICKSBURG

JACKSON

RALEIGH

GALLATIN

BAHALA

HAZLEHURST

BROOKHAVEN

BOGUECHITTO

PORT HUDSON

SUMMIT

MAGNOLIA

CLINTON

OSYKA

GREENSBURG

MAY 2

BATON ROUGE

NEW ORLEANS

ARKANSAS

MISSISSIPPI RIVER

MISSISSIPPI

PEARL RIVER

LOUISIANA

K.G

◄Baxie

◄Randall

AND THE BLUE RAIDERS

---

by CARL G. HODGES

ILLUSTRATED BY

KENNETH CLEMENTS

THE **BOBBS-MERRILL** COMPANY, INC.
A SUBSIDIARY OF HOWARD W. SAMS & CO., INC.
Publishers • INDIANAPOLIS • NEW YORK

Contents

◄ B AXIE
◄ R ANDALL

AND THE BLUE RAIDERS

I.

Disaster in the Clearing

BAXIE RANDALL was unusually tall for his twelve
years and he sat the saddle of the roan mare like a
grown man. He held the reins loosely, his left hand
resting on the saddle horn. His right hand held a
rope halter tied around the neck of Pegasus, standing behind the mare.

Pegasus was a big stallion, his hide as white as
milk. His mane was the color of cornsilk and he was
a full sixteen hands high. Now Pegasus was blowing
a little and pawing at the dust. Baxie knew that he
was just showing off a little for the benefit of the
saddled mare and the three unhaltered ones inside
the split-rail corral.

"Baxie!"

Young Randall shifted his one hundred and thirty pounds in the saddle and looked back at the house. The early morning sun was throwing spots of gold on its cedar-shake roof. His father stood in the dog-trot, the open passageway through the middle of the building. "Have you got everything you'll need, son? We'll never come back this way again."

The little four-room house with the clapboard sides and the cedar-shake roof was the only home he had ever had. Baxie's throat tightened a little. He felt he might cry, as he had done when his mother died the year before. He braced his shoulders and tried to keep the sadness out of his voice as he shouted to his father, "I've got everything. Peg's all ready. Did you remember Mom's Bible?"

Jedediah Randall waved the little pocket Bible and then came out of the dog-trot carrying his rifle. It was a brand-new Henry and he was very proud of it. He was a tall, lean man with a craggy chin. He had blue eyes that could be as merry as a setter pup's or as fiery as a trapped bobcat's. Anyone would have known at a glance that Baxie was his son. They had the same lean, rangy build, the same blue eyes and craggy chin and the same calm manner of speaking.

Jed Randall went into the corral and put the rifle in the saddle boot on the saddled mare. He took a knapsack off the saddle horn and put the Bible in it and then hung the knapsack around his neck by the leather strap. He put his left hand on the saddle-horn and vaulted into the saddle. The mare reared and snorted loudly.

Pegasus pranced and pawed the dirt and snorted.

The elder Randall leaned forward suddenly in the saddle. He put his hand over the mare's muzzle. "Quiet, girl!"

The mare quieted quickly, as if she knew danger was coming.

Then Baxie heard the sounds that had alerted his father, the slap of hoofbeats in deep dust, the odd creak of saddle leather, the clank of equipment. He looked at his father. "They're riding this way! From the south. Do you think they're soldiers?"

"Sssh!" his father uttered. "If they're real soldiers we have no worry, son."

Baxie whispered fearfully, "What if it's Colonel Dark?"

There was no time for the elder Randall to answer. A dozen riders came plunging out of the woods into the clearing. The leader was a brawny, bearded man on a huge black horse. His hat was turned up to one side, with a turkey feather stuck in its band. The riders behind him were dressed in a dozen varieties of clothing. Their clothes and boots as well as their horses were all dust-caked, as if they had been riding a long trail.

The leader reined in his mount. The black horse spread his front legs and put his head down and blew. He was foam-flecked around the shoulders.

Pegasus screamed and reared high on his back legs. His front feet pawed the air. His nostrils flared and showed red against his white hide. Baxie jerked the stallion's halter. "Down, Peg!"

The white stallion went down again on all fours. The leader of the group dug his heels into the black horse. He reined up in front of Jed Randall. "That's a mighty fine horse you've got there, mister. We aim to buy him."

Randall said in his calm way, "The white stallion is not for sale, sir."

"Mister, we got a need for horses. We're requisitioning all you've got for the Confederate States of America. I'm Colonel Dark." His black eyes shone and he put his right hand on the butt of a big pistol.

Baxie said, "You're not a real Colonel! You're just a . . ."

His father said, "I'll do the talking, son."

Baxie said, "Yes, sir."

Colonel Dark wheeled his horse around and faced his men. "Find some rope. Make halters for all the horses. We'll take everything except the mare with foal."

Jed Randall pulled his rifle from the gun boot.

"First I've got to see the color of your money, Colonel." He put a special kind of emphasis on the title of colonel.

Colonel Dark said, "I'll give you a bill of sale, mister. You can trade it for cash at Confederate headquarters."

Randall calmly raised the rifle. "Let's quit playing games, Colonel. My son is right. You're no more a colonel than he is. You have no connection with the army of the Confederacy. You're a guerilla!"

Colonel Dark wheeled the black horse angrily. "Are you calling me a liar, mister?"

"You don't want to buy my horses, Colonel. You are trying to steal them." He held the rifle steady, his eyes alert.

At that instant one of Colonel Dark's men wheeled his horse around hard into Randall's. The mare reared and Randall's rifle discharged harmlessly into the air. The mare reared and wheeled again.

Colonel Dark drew his pistol and fired. The ball struck Randall in the back. His horse came down on all fours with a jolt. Randall tumbled out of the saddle. His body sprawled out in the dust, face down.

Baxie Randall shouted, "Dad!" He jumped from his mount and ran to his father. He was aware of jostling horses and shouting men but he paid little

attention. Dust swirled around them as he knelt by his father's side. "Dad," he sobbed, trying to turn his father's body over.

The elder Randall moaned. He turned his head a little to the side so he could look at his son. His eyes filled with pain.

"Dad. I'm here."

"He shot me in the back. How bad is it?"

Baxie watched the red spot growing rapidly on the back of his father's jacket. He tried to hold back the tears. His father was badly wounded. "A little right of center, Dad. I'll get some bandages and I'll have you fixed up in no time."

His father moaned and raised his body slightly from the dust. Then his right arm bent under him and he collapsed. His chin hit the ground. "My arm's dead, son," he said haltingly. "You start out for La Grange. The Federal cavalry is there. They'll take care of you."

Baxie felt tears in his eyes and he wiped them away with the back of his hand. "We'll both go to La Grange, Dad. I'll bandage you up and then . . ."

He heard hoarse shouts from the direction of the house. Colonel Dark's men had run through it, searching for anything valuable. Now they came out and mounted and ringed their horses about Colonel Dark's black horse.

Inside the doorway of the house Baxie could see

15

fingers of flame licking at the covers of a bed. "Dad, they've set the house on fire!" On impulse he leaped to his feet and began to run toward the blazing house.

One of the guerillas spurred his horse across Baxie's path and swung his rifle. Baxie ducked as quickly as he could but the barrel of the weapon struck his head. He fell in the dust, stunned.

Colonel Dark laughed and spurred his black horse across the ground to where Baxie's father lay. He dismounted and knelt by the elder Randall. He unfastened the wounded man's shirt and pulled off a canvas money belt. "We couldn't find any cash in the house so we knew it was on you. You were pullin' out of here for good. Takin' them horses to the Feds, no doubt. We got better use for them." He opened the money belt and took out a thin sheaf of bills, putting them into his own pocket.

Randall said, coughing, "You . . .! My boy will be left without a cent."

"That's not my worry." Colonel Dark discarded the empty money belt and kicked it away with his boot. He went to his horse and mounted.

Some of his men had driven the Randall mares out of the corral, herding them and the white stallion toward the edge of the clearing. Dark shouted, "We don't want that mare with foal. She can't wear a saddle."

16

His men cut out the mare and she moved over toward the corral fence. Colonel Dark shouted, "Keep the white stallion in front. Them others will follow him. What did that brat call him?"

One of the guerillas, somehow cleaner looking than the rest, answered, "Peg."

"Funny name for a horse."

"He probably meant Pegasus."

"What kind of a name is that?"

"He was a horse in Greek mythology. He had wings. A man named Bellerophon had an idea to ride him right up to heaven but the gods didn't want him to do it so they stung him with a gadfly and . . ."

Colonel Dark stared at him. "Poppycock!" He took off his hat with the turkey feather and waved it in the air. "Let's ride, men! Harper! Walton! Keep that white stallion in front!"

Dark spurred his own black horse and led them galloping out of the clearing. They vanished almost immediately in the cover of the trees. The *clip-clop* of hooves, the creak of saddle leather, the clank of equipment sounded for a short time. Then silence fell.

Baxie wakened with his head throbbing dully. He felt the lump at the back where the guerilla had struck him with the rifle barrel. His fingers touched the still wet smear of blood where the skin was broken.

He forgot all that when he looked around the clearing and saw it emptied of everything but the silent body of his father. He heard a crackling noise and turned. Flames covered the walls of the house and leapt skyward through the roof.

He jumped to his feet and ran toward it. He could feel the heat reaching out from the crackling flames. He ran around the house to a small lean-to that had served as his room.

It was not yet ablaze but flames were licking at its walls. He ran inside, pulled all the covers off his bed, carried them outside and piled them on the ground. He went back again and found a gear box under the bed that he had used as a catchall for his personal belongings. A burning board crashed down from the ceiling and scattered sparks over him. He dragged the gear box out into the clearing under the big oak. He lifted the lid and dug around inside. He found a coil of rope, nearly new.

He took the rope and gathered up the bed covers and hurried across the clearing to his father. He saw the discarded money belt lying on the ground.

Jed Randall twisted around in pain and looked at his son. His voice was little more than a whisper. "Son," he said, "never in the world has any man left a son so little. Colonel Dark took my money, the horses, all but the mare Lucy . . . you'll have nothing." His voice broke. "A twelve-year-old boy,

18

alone . . ." His voice trailed off and he closed his eyes.

Baxie was tearing a clean sheet into narrow strips. He took off his father's jacket and shirt, then brought water from the spring and washed out the wound, binding it up with the clean white cloths. "I've got *you*, Dad. And we've got Lucy and she'll have a colt soon and we'll be back in business. I'll take you to La Grange and one of those cavalry surgeons will dig out this bullet and you'll be good as new again."

Jed Randall reached out and drew his knapsack to him. He took out the Bible and looked at it. "This was your mother's Bible, Baxter. She'd want you to have it."

His real name sounded odd, coming from Father like that. It was his mother's maiden name. Her father had owned a large plantation in Virginia but a fire had destroyed the mansion and wiped out his crops about a year after she had married Jedediah and they had decided to enter the horse breeding business.

Baxie looked at his father and was shocked at the change in him.

His father coughed. His breath was making a queer rattling sound in his throat. "When I go . . . read something out of the Bible over me, will you, son?"

Baxie felt tears welling into his eyes. He turned

his head away so his father could not see his fear. "You're going to be all right, Dad."

Jed Randall pressed the little Bible into his son's hand. He shook his head. "By sundown you'll be an orphan, boy."

2.

Race Against Death!

Baxie caught Lucy and made a rope halter for her. He tied her to the corral fence, close to where his father lay. The mare was twice as large as normal through the barrel and very slow moving. Baxie knew she could never be saddled and should not be ridden. But he was sure that the mare could pull a "travois" without harm to her.

A travois was a litter used by the Indians. He had seen a picture of one once in a book his father had about the Cherokees. It was simply a pair of long poles fastened to a horse like the shafts of a wagon. The ends of the poles dragged on the ground behind the horse. Blankets fastened between the poles would allow belongings, or a woman or a child, or a

21

wounded man, to be transported from one place to another. Baxie was sure they could make the trip to La Grange safely with his father riding on a travois.

He cut down two small straight saplings and trimmed off all the branches. This gave him two slender but strong poles about fifteen feet long. He put the poles on the ground parallel to each other and about thirty inches apart. At one end of the poles he spread the blankets and bedcovers, fastening them with wooden strips nailed into the poles to keep the materials from ripping. He used a length of rope between the two pole ends so the addition of his father's weight would not spread the poles or tear the blankets loose.

Next he made a harness of rope for Lucy. He put it around her powerful shoulders so he could lash the free ends of the poles to it like the shafts of a wagon. He was pretty proud of his handiwork as he stood back and looked it over.

He ran over to his father and knelt beside him. "Dad, I can't lift you, but if you can help yourself a little, we can get you on the travois."

Jed Randall coughed. Pain twisted his features. He tried to crawl but he just did not have the strength. "I can't do it, Baxter. Just let me rest here."

Baxie said, "We'll get you on the travois, Dad, one way or another."

He finally did it by rolling his father's body over and over until he was parallel with the travois. Here his father could grasp the poles, and with Baxie's help, he managed to pull his body onto the blankets. He stretched out with a tired sigh. He coughed again. It still made that queer sound in his throat, as if something was loose and rattling there. "I'm right proud of you, son," he managed to say.

"Don't talk, Dad. Just rest. Next thing you know you'll be in La Grange and the cavalry doctor can take care of you."

Baxie untied Lucy from the corral fence. The mare turned her head and looked at the queer contraption behind her. Then she looked at Baxie with her huge round eyes and nuzzled him. He took her halter and led her toward the edge of the clearing. A crackling, tearing sound made him stop and look back.

The walls of his home were collapsing into the middle of the dog-trot. Sparks scattered. Smoke twisted upward into the circle of blue sky above the clearing.

He braced his shoulders resolutely. Leading the fat mare, which he knew was liable to give birth to a foal at any moment and thus be useless to them, he went down a lane toward the main road. He could smell the fragrance of peach and plum blossoms as he moved through a grove of fruit trees and the travois made tracks through thousands of fallen petals.

The main road was little more than a double rut worn down through the years but he knew he would have to follow it to reach La Grange and find an Army surgeon who could get the bullet out of his father's body.

The poles of the travois were narrower than the ruts in the road and often one pole would trail in a deep rut while the other was on high ground. When this happened the elder Randall was thrown sideways and jolted badly. His wound began to bleed and it soaked the bandages and the blankets. His face grew red as his fever rose. His eyes became glassy and once a moan was torn from his lips.

Baxie said, "Whoa, Lucy," and dropped her halter and went back to kneel in the road beside the travois. "We'll make it all right, Dad. Just a few more miles and we'll be in La Grange."

His father smiled weakly. "Son, we haven't traveled more than a couple of miles. La Grange is still a long way off." His voice faded away. He looked at his son proudly. He licked his lips and brushed his fingers across his eyes with a tired motion. "I could sure do with a drink of water, son."

They moved finally through a copse of redbud and dogwood and came out in a small clearing. There was an acre of scant, half-tilled cotton and a tumble-down shack. A well was behind the shack. It was dry when Baxie let down the bucket. The shack itself was deserted. Baxie said, "The owners are gone. Maybe they've pulled out to join the Rebs."

The elder Randall said, "Or else Colonel Dark robbed them of everything they had, too."

They plodded on for an hour without finding water. There were no signs of life anywhere in the hard, dry land. Lucy's flanks were wet with sweat. Froth covered her shoulders where the travois harness was tied.

They passed several dry washes cutting the road. Once they had been creeks running full. Now they were ditches ankle deep in rippled white sand. Jed Randall said, "It was a dry winter, dry spring. One of these days, though, the clouds will open up and . . ." He stopped suddenly and lifted his eyes to the sky and called, "Pegasus!"

Baxie stopped and ran around to him. "Dad!"

Jed Randall stared at him. His eyes were glassy and seemed to be unable to focus on his son. He seemed to be watching something that was not visible to Baxie. Then just as suddenly his eyes focused and he laughed weakly. "I guess I was sort of thinking of that big white horse of ours, son. If Pegasus could fly to heaven, I sort of wish I could get him to fly to La Grange." His cracked lips spread

25

in a grin. "Pegasus is gone . . . so I can't fly." His eyes grew wild again. "Get Pegasus back, boy. Get Pegasus back!" He closed his eyes and slumped sideways on the travois as one of the poles dropped off into a deep rut.

Baxie knelt down closer. His father was breathing heavily now and that queer rattle in his throat was more pronounced. Baxie held his father's wrist for a moment. He could feel no pulse. He bent his head and put his ear to his father's chest. He was relieved when he heard the faint thump of the heart and felt the rise and fall of the chest.

Baxie got up. He went around and got Lucy's halter and they resumed their plodding progress. "We've got to find water, Lucy."

Lucy blew and looked around at him with her huge, gentle eyes. He said, "Get along, Lucy. It'll be easier going now. We're in the short-leaf pines. We . . . there it is! Water!"

Around a brief outcrop of sandstone he saw the trickle of water as it spilled across the road. It made a little pool and gurgled away through the cool, shady pine woods.

Baxie stopped the travois. He knelt, filled his hat with water and managed to carry it back to his father. The wounded man drank and smiled gratefully. Then he bathed his father's face with the cold water and let him drink some more.

26

Lucy was standing with her forefeet in the pool, drinking and then blowing with pleasure.

Baxie would have liked to splash in the water himself but there was no time. He knew that a doctor's care was absolutely necessary, and soon. He took Lucy's halter and began to lead her across the water.

A voice, deep and ringing, shouted from behind the sandstone outcrop, "Hold it, boy!"

All Baxie could see was the black barrel of a carbine, jutting out at him. He was startled when a Union soldier stepped out cautiously from behind the rock, his carbine leveled. The soldier was tall, thin and blond and he had a reddish moustache that looked rough as a currycomb. He wore a dark blue blouse and light blue trousers stuck in black boots, with a revolver in a holster on his right hip. His blue cap had a black visor with crossed sabers on it. His uniform was piped with yellow braid.

Baxie said, "You're a Federal cavalryman. I'm glad to see you."

The soldier said, "Corporal Dan Marksbury. Company B. Seventh Illinois Cavalry. What you got on that litter? What's your name? Where you from? Where you think you're going?"

Baxie hurriedly told him the events of the morning. "My dad ought to have a doctor real quick."

Marksbury said, "So Colonel Dark caused all this,

eh? He's been shootin' and robbin' all through this short-leaf country. The Rebs got no use for him, either, although he always tries to pass himself off as one of them. He's slippery as an eel."

"He stole all our horses, including a white stallion, Pegasus. He burned our house. He shot my father. We've got to get my father to a doctor."

The cavalryman grinned. "I can beat that. I'll bring a doctor. La Grange is about half a mile north. I'll ride in and fetch an ambulance for your dad. You wait here."

Marksbury ran behind the outcrop and was gone for a moment. There was a stamping and snorting, then he came riding out on a big black horse. He galloped rapidly down the road in the direction of La Grange.

Baxie led Lucy the rest of the way across the water and stopped the travois. He untied the harness from around Lucy's shoulders and allowed the poles of the travois to drop to the ground. He did his best to make his father comfortable. He gave him another drink of water and bathed his face. His father's skin felt very hot. His eyes were wild again and he mumbled, "You go after Pegasus, son. You got to get Pegasus!"

Baxie said, "I will, Dad." His father closed his eyes then and he held tight to Baxie's hand as if he were in a lot of pain from his wound.

Within a few minutes Baxie heard the clop of horses' hooves and the rattle of wheels from down the road. Then Marksbury rode up on his big black horse and dismounted. A short distance behind him was an ambulance wagon pulled by two horses and driven by a fat Negro. Beside the driver was a man in a blue uniform with brass buttons who looked very stern and military. He wore a black hat with a yellow cord on it. He had eyeglasses with a black ribbon, and sideburns curved along the side of his jaw.

He climbed down from the ambulance and said to the Negro, "Back it around, Bertman, so the back step's as close as you can get it."

The driver clucked to the horses and they wheeled in the narrow road and turned the ambulance around. Then he and Marksbury climbed up the step in back of the ambulance wagon and lifted down a stretcher that was fitted on the seat on the left side.

They put the stretcher on the ground beside the travois. The doctor bent over Jed Randall. He felt his pulse, then listened to his chest. He gently pushed one of Jed Randall's eyelids back.

The doctor sighed heavily and slowly got to his feet. He looked at Baxie and put his hand on the boy's shoulder. "Lad," he said, "I'm sorry. Your father is dead."

3.

Be Out of This Camp by Sundown!

The doctor, Captain Goodall, invited Baxie to
ride into camp on the front seat of the ambulance.
With his father's body behind him, covered with a
blanket, Baxie sat between Captain Goodall and
the big Negro driver. Corporal Dan Marksbury led
the procession. Lucy was tied to the back step of
the ambulance wagon.

Tears wanted to come to Baxie's eyes but he re-
fused to let them. He was as much alone as any
grown man had ever been and he made up his mind
to try to act like a man. He squared his shoulders
and looked at Captain Goodall and said, "When we
bury my father, sir, I would like to read over him
from my mom's Bible, like he asked me to."

31

Captain Goodall put his hand on Baxie's shoulder and smiled at him. "That you shall, boy. You just keep your eyes open around the bend in the road. Just at the edge of camp is a big magnolia. It's a right pretty spot. The grass is growing deep and green there and the wild songbirds will sing for your father."

Just then they turned a bend in the road and Baxie had his first glimpse of La Grange, Tennessee. It had probably been a pretty little town but now it was crowded with tents and other temporary shelters for soldiers and horses and equipment. The smell of leather and horses and dead camp fires hung over the place, mixed with the scent of spring-blooming flowers.

The little houses were all neat and tidy but their fences had long ago gone into soldiers' campfires. Gardens had been trampled into dust by the horses and at the front porch of one white house a dozen cavalry mounts trampled the stump of what had once been a lilac bush. Odd, conical tents filled most of the open spaces in the streets and between the houses.

They were Sibley tents, Captain Goodall informed Baxie, that had been invented before the war by a Union officer who was now serving as a General in the Army of the Confederacy. Each could hold a dozen soldiers with room for a fire in the middle so the soldiers could sleep around it with their feet to the fire like the spokes of a wheel.

Right now they didn't need a fire; it was warm spring and the apple, plum and pear trees were loaded with blossoms. The sight made Baxie think of the fruit trees that had grown around their own little clearing. Near the porch of a house Baxie saw the golden color of a forsythia bush with a hound dog dozing under it. His mother had tended a bush like that.

The town looked as if it housed a thousand civilians and to Baxie, who was used to his little home and a horse corral in a clearing, the camp seemed as big and busy as New York, which he had read about in a book.

To the east of the town there was a college building on top of a knoll but it had been made into a hospital and soldiers limped around it on the grass, using homemade crutches. On the north side of the town there was another rise and on top of it was a Ladies' Seminary. Baxie didn't know what a Ladies' Seminary was, but it sounded important.

Captain Goodall pointed to a spot beside the big magnolia tree, perhaps twenty feet back from the road. "There's the place, boy. Buried there, your father will sleep close to God."

"That will be fine, sir."

Corporal Marksbury and Bertman got shovels out

of the ambulance and dug a grave in the middle of the grassy plot by the magnolia tree. They carefully placed Randall's body in it, wrapped in a canvas, after removing his few personal things from his clothes and giving them to Baxie.

Baxie walked to the head of the grave. He opened the Bible to a page his father had once marked with a pencil. In a clear voice, struggling to hold back the tears, he read the passage from *John:14.*

"Let not your heart be troubled: ye believe in God, believe also in me.

"In my Father's house are many mansions: if it were not so, I would have told you. I go to prepare a place for you.

"And if I go and prepare a place for you, I will come again, and receive you unto myself; that where I am, there ye may be also."

Only then, did Baxie break down and cry.

Captain Goodall hugged the boy's body and said, "Cry, boy, it'll do you good. Get it all out. Tomorrow is always another day for all of God's children. You don't understand that now, but you will."

The first shovelful of earth fell on Randall's canvas-wrapped body and the boy turned away, sobbing and holding tightly to the hand of Captain Goodall.

The Captain asked, "Have you had anything to eat, boy?"

"Dad fixed us some flapjacks and eggs for break-
fast."

Marksbury's rough face relaxed into a smile and
his nose spread over his face looking as if he had
often had it punched in brawls. "You can mess with
me, boy. Hardtack and beef stew."

The doctor chuckled. "Beef stew? You boys in
Company B throw anything loose into a pot and
call it beef stew. I'll wager there's chicken necks
and pig's feet and fish tails in the pot, too."

Marksbury's laugh bubbled out of him. He
seemed to be young, but Baxie got the impression
that this soldier could take care of himself. "It im-
proves the flavor, Captain."

Suddenly he changed the subject and stared at
Baxie. "You and me went through the same thing,
boy. My ma and pa died when the *Henry Clay* hit
a snag in the Mississippi River off Oquawka and
sank in thirty feet of water with a hundred excur-
sion riders aboard her. We had a farm in Warren
County and Dad was sharecroppin' corn. This ex-
cursion boat come along to Davenport, over in
Ioway, and the folks was wild to go on it on account
of it was their anniversary. They didn't have money
for all the family so they left me with my grandma
that afternoon . . . a year later Granny died and I
been fighting my own battles ever since. You got to
learn how, boy. You got to learn how to do your

own riding, your own shooting, you got to earn your own living. I did it, boy. You can do it, too."

Captain Goodall said, "You earned your chevron's in this man's army, Corporal. But you can't ride in the cavalry and take a twelve-year-old boy to raise."

"Nobody has to raise me," Baxie said, sharply. "Last of all, this army. I'm riding south. The last thing Dad asked me was to find Pegasus. I figure Colonel Dark is riding south so that's where I'm heading. I'm going to find Pegasus."

"What are you going to use for money, boy?" Marksbury asked. "You have to eat. You got to have a horse to ride. That nag of yours is so fat with foal you couldn't get your legs around her belly."

A group of riders swept out of a lane, led by a tall, bearded man with a fancy hat turned up on one side. He wore white gauntlets and his uniform was decorated with yellow braid and brass buttons. He had a big pistol in a black holster and a saber swung by his side. He rode as if he had been born in the saddle.

Baxie's eyes focused on the big claybank horse the officer rode. He gave a low whistle and then he called, "Bonnie! Bonnie, girl!"

The claybank stopped so suddenly that the rider was almost thrown from the saddle. The horse left the road and came across the grass to Baxie. She put her muzzle down by his jacket pocket and neighed. Baxie put his arm around her neck and hugged her. "Bonnie!"

The officer smiled down at the boy through his heavy beard. "You seem on better terms with this piece of horseflesh than I am, boy."

"My dad raised her, sir. She's out of Maryland by Geography. She's four years old now. I remember her record from Dad's book. Geography was the stallion Dad had before he got Pegasus. Dad sold Bonnie to the Army last winter. A Lieutenant Lancaster bought seven horses from Dad that time." He stroked the horse's neck and she looked at him with her brown, gentle eyes. She nuzzled him again. "Bonnie always liked me, sir. I used to feed her apples all the time from the big tree in the clearing by our corral."

The officer frowned and said to Captain Goodall, "Is this a civilian aide of yours, Captain?"

"No, sir." Captain Goodall went on to explain the circumstances of the elder Randall's death and his burial under the magnolia tree.

The bearded officer said, "Buy the boy's horse for a reasonable sum or else trade even. Then ship him home to his nearest relatives."

"But, Colonel . . ."

"No *buts*. We break camp at dawn. Orders have gone out. Oats in the nose bags and five days' rations in haversacks. The rations to last ten days.

Double rations of salt. Forty rounds of ammunition per man."

"But, Colonel . . ."

"That will be all, Captain."

Captain Goodall saluted and stepped aside and said, "Yes, sir."

The officer put spurs to Bonnie and led his companions off at a brisk canter. They vanished into a copse of trees near the little depot. Baxie said, "He'd be better-humored if he looked at the world through fewer whiskers."

Marksbury said, "That was Colonel Hatch. He's top man of the Second Ioway Cavalry but the gossip is he's going to be our brigadier general when we finally start riding some place. He was a lumber man . . . had a business in Muscatine, Ioway. He happened to be in Washington on business the day war broke out and he volunteered to help guard the White House. He got himself a lieutenant's commission for that and he hurried back home and helped to organize the Second Ioway."

Baxie asked, "Who were the others? They looked mighty important."

"Colonel Prince of the Seventh Illinois. He's my commanding officer. He was a lawyer before the war, in a little town named Quincy on the Mississippi River 'way up north past Cairo some place. The others were Major Blackburn and Captain

Forbes. Forbes is the big man of Company B." He smiled with his rough features at the young boy. "War is too important for us to be saddled with boys that ain't dry behind the ears yet."

Baxie, stung by the words, answered, "Sounds to me like you're makin' yourself mighty big for your britches. I'll wager you don't even know what you're fighting this war about."

"I don't have to know, boy. As long as Abe Lincoln knows, that's enough for me. Gettin' back to you, the Colonel says you get shipped off to your nearest relatives."

"I've got no relatives any more. Besides, what am I going to do with Lucy?"

"You heard the Colonel. We'll trade you a horse for her or we'll buy her for a nominal sum."

"Nominal? If that means little," Baxie said, "I don't agree to it. Almost any day now Lucy will be a bargain. She'll be worth two horses instead of one. Her colt will be one of Pegasus'."

Captain Goodall interrupted with a smile, "You've got a point there, son. Anyhow, I'll give you an order on the quartermaster. He'll trade with you or buy for cash. Is that satisfactory?"

Marksbury said, "That's a good offer, boy. You'd better grab it."

Baxie smiled at the doctor. "I think I'll trade, doctor."

39

"Good. But don't forget. Orders are for you to be out of this camp by sundown. The Colonel gave those orders and I have to obey them." He put out his big hand to Baxie. "Promise?"

Baxie frowned. "Yes, sir," he said. He tried to act confident and sure of himself but inside fears and doubts were mounting. The world was a big place for a twelve-year-old boy to be alone in.

He turned to Marksbury. "I'm sorry I was so dauncey, Corporal. I didn't mean to act like a smart aleck. I guess it's just that . . ."

Marksbury grinned at him. "You're scared. I know just how you feel, boy."

4.

Forty Dead Men in Cartridge Boxes

Marksbury led Baxie down a street of tents to the quartermaster wagon of Company B, Seventh Illinois Cavalry. The sergeant on duty was a dour Scot named MacDougall, who had piercing blue eyes and a thatch of curly gray hair. "Me feet hurt," he complained, with his burry accent, "and what do ye two rogues want with Sandy?" He put his eyes on the horses they were leading. "Me thinks it is the glue factory ye're wanting."

Marksbury said, trying to act like an old and experienced trooper, "Sarge, Captain Goodall says to pay this man for his horse, or trade for her. He says he'll sign the papers."

"Who said that?"

"Captain Goodall."

"Sure, and he's the one dug the ball out of me carcass at Shiloh. Anything the good doctor wants the good doctor can have, says I." He grunted in Baxie's direction. "What do ye think this nag is worth, boy?"

"I'm not a boy, Sergeant. Lucy is not a nag. As anyone can see now, very soon she will be two horses instead of one. So I won't sell her. I want a cavalry horse to ride, and more to boot."

Sergeant MacDougall's eyes crinkled at the corners. He looked at Marksbury and winked. "A canny lad, this." He turned again to Baxie. "And what might ye want to boot?"

"First, a saddle. Then a carbine like the corporal's, with a magazine in the stock. A cartridge box and ammunition. A haversack, an axe, a knife and a camp kettle. A poncho, and a blanket I can sleep in or make a tent of. I'm riding south and I'll have to travel fast."

MacDougall said, "That's a lot to boot for one fat nag."

"Not one horse, Sergeant. Two horses."

MacDougall waggled his head. "A hard bargain ye drive, lad. But have it your way. Only me thinks Captain Forbes will be havin' me hide when he hears of it."

The sergeant led the way to a copse of trees near

42

the railroad depot where a long rope had been strung between a tree and the depot office and dozens of horses had been tethered. "These are the remounts for Company B, lad. Take your pick."

Baxie and Marksbury walked down the rear of the long line of mounts. Marksbury stopped behind a tall, rangy black with one white foot. "This one might be a sister to my Ebony, Randall. She looks like she could go from here to some place else mighty fast."

Baxie said, "I don't want to run any quarter races. I might have to follow Colonel Dark and Pegasus all the way to the Gulf of Mexico. I want good wind and stamina mostly." He pointed to a small roan with a patch of white over her left eye which made her seem to be permanently winking. "That one's for me and I'll call her Belle. For Bellerophon going after Pegasus, like in the stories Dad used to read to me."

"Ye've picked well, lad." MacDougall untied the roan from the rope and gave her halter to Baxie. Then he led them back to the quartermaster wagon that had the name of the company and the regiment stenciled on the side. He got the equipment Baxie had asked for, listed it all in his records and turned it over, item by item.

Baxie put the saddle pad on the roan all by himself. He needed help to lift the heavy cavalry saddle on his new mount. He cinched the girth fairly tight. He ran his finger between the webbing and the roan's belly to be sure it was just right. Loose enough for the horse to move and breathe easily and yet tight enough so that the saddle wouldn't slip when he mounted. He rolled his axe, knife, fry pan and cup inside the big blanket and fastened it in a tight roll behind his saddle.

He put his cartridge box at his waist and then he regarded the haversack. "There's nothing to put in it. It's a waste of time to carry that thing around."

"No," Marksbury said, "it makes a good pillow when it's stuffed with leaves and when you hit the road you'll be glad it's stuffed with hardtack and coffee beans."

Baxie slipped his arms into the straps so the empty haversack rested on his back. Marksbury made a stepping stone of his hands and Baxie took the reins and got into the saddle. He had only time enough to shove his right foot into the stirrup before his head snapped back as if his entire body had been pulled away from it.

"Hi-ah! Hi-ah!" yelled Dan Marksbury.

"Bless me soul," the Scotchman yelled, "but that there roan is a stemwinder!"

Baxie realized now that he had picked a mount that was not entirely saddle-broken. The roan pin-wheeled and sunfished and bucked all over a half

44

acre trying to dislodge the human annoyance on her back.

Baxie grinned from ear to ear as the critter literally changed ends under him. He took off his hat and rapped her flank with it. "Come on, Belle!" he yelled. "Get it out of your system, girl! You and me are going to be pals for a long time so we might as well get used to each other. Buck your fool head off, Belle! Dad taught me to ride rougher ones than you!"

The roan cocked her head back at him. The eye with the white patch gave her a rakish look. Then she began another series of sidesteps and sunfishes. She broke into a dead run down the company street. She upset a stack of arms and scattered the ashes of a camp fire with her flying hooves. Soldiers yelled as she flashed by them. Just as suddenly as she had started her run, she stopped.

Her forefeet plowed deep tracks in the earth. But Baxie, grinning, was still on her back. He was beating her flank with his hat and yelling, "Come on, Belle, you can do better than that!"

Belle tried to. She ran. She braked again. She changed ends in the air. Baxie still sat on her back. And now other cavalrymen, aroused from daytime dozings and attracted by the shouts of Baxie and Marksbury and MacDougall, were gathering to watch the struggle between the boy and the horse.

One old soldier said, "MacDougall's been tryin' to palm that roan off on somebody ever since Christmas. But that boy sticks to her like a cockleburr."

"Stay on her, boy!" another cried.

"That's the way to ride, lad! You showed that roan up good and proper! Old Sandy, too! You got the better of both of them!"

The white-eyed roan was foam-flecked and breathing hard. She gave one final, desperate, twisting leap. She came down on all fours with a jolt that should have unseated almost anybody. She turned

her head and looked back. That pesky boy was still there. She looked at him with that white eye. Baxie would have sworn that she winked at him.

Her battle was over and she stood quietly. Baxie knew that she was ready to obey her master's will from now on.

A tall, bearded officer came out of a Sibley tent. He was lean as a fence rail and looked tough as a thong of rawhide but he had a friendly gleam in his eyes. He came up to the group gathered around the roan. The men all saluted. He was Captain Henry Forbes of Company B, Seventh Illinois Cavalry. He grinned and said, "Sergeant, it looks like you've finally got the roan off your remount rope."

MacDougall grew a little red in the face. "I had me a wee bit of an idea the lad could fork him all right."

Forbes looked at Marksbury. "Who is this boy?"

Marksbury told him. He also said that Baxie would be heading south, hunting the white stallion, Pegasus.

Captain Forbes said, "Randall, that rascal Dark knows the forests and the swamps like an otter. You'll never catch up with the likes of him."

Baxie said, "Sir, I know all the territory between here and Baton Rouge like I know my own face. Dad and I bought and sold and traded horses up and down the whole stretch. We even traded some

47

with the Parrish Brothers in New Orleans. I can get along. I can live off the land."

Forbes smiled. "Baton Rouge? New Orleans? Well, well!" He turned to MacDougall. "Seeing as this young man has no living relatives his Uncle Sam hereby adopts him. Put him in a uniform. He can ride south with us. Maybe he can find this Pegasus he's looking for and be a guide for us at the same time."

Marksbury said, "Beggin' your pardon, sir, I guess I'd better tell you something. Colonel Hatch ordered the boy to be out of this camp by sundown."

Captain Forbes chuckled softly. "I didn't hear a word you said, Corporal. Give this boy a haircut, give him a bath, put a uniform on him. He can sign his enlistment papers in the morning."

Marksbury saluted smartly. "Yes, sir," he said.

Baxie said, "I don't see why I should fight for either side in this ruckus. I'm not mad at anybody. I know a lot of people south of here. They don't grow horns and I don't want to shoot them. I only want to find Pegasus."

Captain Forbes stared at him sternly. "I'm not going to be responsible for a twelve-year-old orphan traipsing over the country looking for a horse. As of now, boy, you're practically a ward of the government and you'll obey orders. Do you understand that?"

Baxie wasn't sure he understood but he was frightened by Captain Forbes and he nodded his head silently. "That's better," Captain Forbes said, and walked away.

Baxie drew his new uniform from MacDougall. He put his mother's Bible in the pocket of his new blue wool shirt. The perky blue cap with the crossed sabres on it tilted forward a little on his head, almost making him look like a veteran soldier. The yellow piping and the brass buttons on his blue jacket seemed suddenly to change the boy into a man. With his new shoes and their heavy soles Baxie stood within an inch as tall as his new-found friend.

He still didn't want to fight anybody but he was proud of his soldierly appearance when, before daylight on the morning of April 17, 1863, he followed Dan Marksbury to the Sibley tent where Captain Forbes had his headquarters. A sentry admitted the two and they found the Captain studying a large map laid out on a wooden table top.

Captain Forbes got a printed form from a pile on a cabinet. Baxie signed his name to the paper where the captain indicated. The latter shook his hand and said, gravely, "You are now a private in B Company, Seventh Illinois Cavalry, First Brigade, General U.S. Grant's Army of the Tennessee. Congratulations, boy."

The captain now turned to Marksbury. "Corporal, you will take Private Randall to the Headquarters house. Colonel Benjamin Grierson has just returned from his furlough. *He* is in command of this brigade instead of Colonel Hatch. He wants to talk to Randall. Take him there at once."

In the half-dark a trembling Baxie followed Dan Marksbury through the stirring camp to a white house near the railroad depot. A sentry on the porch admitted them when Marksbury explained their errand. They went into a front room that held only a table and a sofa. The walls were covered with hanging maps. They stood, ill at ease, for a long time.

Finally the door opened from a rear room. A gangling officer with black hair and a spade-shaped beard came into the room. His uniform was fancy but wrinkled a little as if he might have lounged in it. The officer moved easily. He was lean and wiry and his eyes were bright and alive. He greeted Baxie by putting out his hand. "You're the Randall boy, I take it. I'm sorry to hear about your father."

Baxie swallowed in the presence of a great man who could command a whole army of soldiers. "Yes, sir," he said.

"I'm Colonel Ben Grierson," the officer said. "I think I knew your father. We bought some horses from him last winter. I offer my condolences." He shook the boy's hand solemnly, then greeted Marksbury. "Captain Forbes says you know the country south of here very well, Randall. All the way to Baton Rouge, I think he said."

"Yes, sir," was all that Baxie could say.

Colonel Grierson chuckled and put his hand on Baxie's shoulder. "I was a little scared, son, when I put on my first uniform. It was back in Ohio when I was a boy and I was in the Ohio militia. I got over it. So will you." He paused, and his glance took in both soldiers. "Randall, you will ride with Corporal Marksbury in the advance scouts of Lieutenant Lancaster. You will mount picket with the Corporal. The Corporal will keep his eye on you and take care of you. Your knowledge of the terrain will be very valuable to this command once we penetrate enemy territory."

Baxie felt his face redden under the Colonel's gaze. "I don't want to kill anybody, Colonel Grierson, sir. I just want to find my horse. About the North and the South . . . I guess both sides think they're right."

Colonel Grierson moved over to the sofa and sat down on it and his keen eyes regarded Baxie intently. "Son," he said, "I am not a man of battle. But sometimes a man has a job to do." He looked at his hands, studying his long, supple fingers. "Two years ago I was teaching and composing music, organizing bands. For a time I ran a general store in

51

a little Illinois River town of Meredosia. I guess I wasn't much of a success at either one but my wife and I were happy and we got by." He sighed. "Sometimes a man . . . or a nation . . . has to fight for the things they believe in, whether they want to or not."

Baxie said, "I guess maybe the Rebels feel the same way."

"They probably do," Colonel Grierson said, "but in any conflict such as this only one side can be right. I was convinced of that several years ago by the tall and bearded man who is in the White House now."

"You knew Abraham Lincoln?" Baxie asked, awe-struck.

The Colonel smiled. "He stayed at our house in Meredosia one night after he'd made a speech. That was the year he was debating with Stephen A. Douglas up and down our state. Lincoln was on the right track then . . . he's on the right track now. Slavery is, was, and always will be morally wrong. No man has the right to enslave another . . . or to keep him enslaved. It's a matter of *freedom*. That's why we're fighting, boy. And I guess that's why, when Abe Lincoln asked for volunteers, I marched from Jacksonville all the way down to Cairo and why I served as an aide to General Prentiss without pay. Freedom is everybody's business."

Baxie was impressed by the commander's sincerity. "Yes, sir," he said. In spite of himself his heart began to beat faster and a sort of thrill tingled his spine. This man reminded him of his father and a feeling of pride in him and in his country filled him to overflowing.

5.

Beware of Ambush!

At the break of dawn on Friday, April 17, 1863, Baxie Randall, age 12, and Corporal Dan Marksbury, age 27, sat a roan and a black at the head of a long column of two's. B Company of the Seventh Illinois Cavalry was ready to ride.

The horses fretted. Saddles creaked as troopers shifted their weight in the stirrups. Carbines and sabres rattled. Soldiers whispered in excitement.

The company filled a clearing in the short-leaf pines just south of the little town, on the east road. Behind them, and on the west road, which ran parallel, stretched other companies, other riders, all ignorant of where they were going but eager to start. Most of them felt, as Baxie and Dan did, that they were heading for Columbus, Mississippi, to wreck the Rebel railroad there and then dash back to the safety of their base before the Rebels could learn of their coming and ambush them with superior numbers.

It was a beautiful morning. Sun slanted through the trees making the dust from the horses' hooves glint like sparkling jewels. The short-leafs were green but back at the edge of the little town the fruit trees were all in bloom, birds sang and the ground was carpeted with soft, lush grass. War had the air of a picnic on this April morning.

There was a ripple of excitement in the columns behind the two boys. A big bay horse came down the line, prancing a little. Its rider was Captain Henry Forbes. On the other side of the columns were others of the Captain's staff.

The Captain reined in the bay and made a sign to one of his lieutenants with his gauntleted hand. The Lieutenant, whose name was Lancaster, was a cheerful, smiling man whom Baxie remembered because of his visit last winter on the horse buying expedition. He raised his arm, then wheeled his horse slowly down the line. As he passed Baxie he smiled at the boy and gave him a wink. "Welcome, soldier." Baxie felt all warm inside as he grinned and nodded.

Lieutenant Lancaster got out in front of the column, wheeled his horse and looked at his little advance squad. "No bugles this morning, boys. Just follow me. Pass the word."

Quietly, at least as quietly as 1,700 horses and men could move, the Seventh Illinois Cavalry headed south. They were aiming at the heart of the Confederacy, this First Brigade of Blue Raiders. Men and horses coiled through the forest like a huge blue caterpillar with brass buttons.

Lieutenant Lancaster came back and held his horse even with Baxie's mount. "Sorry to hear about your father, soldier. I liked him a lot. Somebody, somehow will catch up with Colonel Dark and make him pay for his crimes."

Marksbury said, "Colonel Grierson is our brigadier now. I never heard the likes."

Lieutenant Lancaster said, very quietly, "Of what?"

"Of Colonel Grierson leading a cavalry raid. He's got no use for horses. He was kicked in the face by a pony when he was a boy and his face got all scarred up. That's why he grew that full beard. He'd much rather play a piano than ride a horse."

The Lieutenant said, "It's not how he handles horses that makes a good commander. It's how he handles men. Don't pass on gossip, boys." He went up front, smiling.

Within an hour the long line of troops had crossed the state line from Tennessee into Mississippi. Travelling at the standard cavalry rate of three miles an hour they moved steadily south. Each hour they halted approximately five minutes to rest their mounts.

The country was flattening out a little now. Occasionally, they would pass farmhouses set back in trees behind split rail fences that were in poor repair.

They stopped at noon for a quick meal. Each squad of troopers ate as a unit. One trooper was delegated to care for the horses. Two got the materials for a small fire and others brewed coffee for the squad. Hardtack was washed down with strong coffee. Some of the troopers ate fruit or cookies that had been stored in their haversacks. They were so well organized, that only half an hour was needed to feed nearly two thousand men and horses.

Shortly after the noon stop they reached a crossroads with which Baxie was very familiar. He knew the road from here headed directly south into the little town of Ripley. He wondered if he would be able to find any trace of Colonel Dark and Pegasus in Ripley.

They forded a small creek and allowed their mounts to drink. They passed a large plantation on the west side of the road. The buildings seemed deserted, the crops untilled. A dog burst from the yard, yelping at them. He was gaunt and unkempt, and he scurried into the timber after a while. They saw no other signs of life.

Marksbury said, "Baxie, I don't like this. It ain't natural that we've ridden fifteen miles into Rebel territory and we haven't seen a livin' soul. Those Rebs, I'll wager, are busy right now settin' a trap for us. They'll suck us in as far as they think we'll go, and then, *blooie!* they'll come down on us with guns blazin'." He gave a quick glance into the trees through which they were moving at the moment. "I got a scary feeling in the middle of my back. Like maybe one of those Rebs was drawin' a bead on me with a squirrel rifle."

Baxie reined Belle up suddenly. The roan's ears pointed backward, as if warning her rider. Baxie said, "There's a wagon coming up ahead. Up around that bend in the road somewhere."

The Corporal said, reining up his mount, "Maybe you got ears like a rabbit, Baxie, but I don't hear a thing. Are you getting scary, too? I don't hear horses. You can't have a wagon without horses."

Baxie said, "Down here you can, Corporal. Oxen. They move very quietly. And they're not shod."

At that moment two oxen rounded the bend in the road ahead. They came forward with their odd, sideward shuffle. They made no noise in the deep dust. The wheels of the homemade wagon they pulled made little squeaking sounds. The driver on the seat, a young fellow in jeans and a butternut jacket and plumed hat, was dozing, unaware that he was driving straight into the van of a raiding cavalry unit.

The lieutenant in the lead cried, "Hold it, Butternut!" calling him by the term often applied to Rebel soldiers and civilians alike because of the homemade cloth used in jackets and trousers they wore.

The young driver, startled and scared, dropped his reins as if to leap from the wagon and bolt through the trees. The riders, including Baxie and Corporal Marksbury, closed in on him, carbines ready. The driver stared at the guns and sank back on his seat.

One of the cavalrymen said, "Johnny Reb, that's a mighty perky hat you got there." He picked it off the boy's head and then spurred his horse down the road, yelling exultantly. B Company came to a halt, enjoying the respite.

Presently Colonel Benjamin Grierson appeared, along with Colonel Edward Prince, who was the commanding officer of the Seventh Illinois. "Why are we stopping here?" Before anyone could reply the young oxen driver began to complain bitterly about the theft of his hat.

"Where did you get a plumed hat, boy?" the Colonel asked. "Plumed hats don't go with the rest of your outfit."

"I won it at a housewarmin' last fall, at the Weatherall's down Pontotoc way."

Colonel Prince said, taking out his wallet and giving the boy a two-dollar bill, "That's more than your hat was worth. But this army does not steal personal belongings. Pull your wagon off the road and let these troops pass. If you tell anybody we have come this way I'll have my men cut out your tongue with a dull knife." Then he smiled at the boy with disarming warmth. "Understand?"

The boy was staring at the money in his hand. It seemed to fascinate him; it was probably the largest amount he had ever owned at one time.

A trooper said, "Colonel Grierson, sir, maybe we ought to take him along with us to keep him from warnin' the Rebs."

Colonel Grierson said, "He's headed north and we're going south. If we can't outrun these oxen, we'll never get to cut any railroads, will we?" The Colonel turned to Baxie and gave him a warm smile. "You are familiar with this part of the country?"

"Yes, sir. Dad and I lived about four miles from here, off to the west. That's where we raised horses. Until Colonel Dark . . ."

Colonel Grierson said, "Did you ever see this oxen driver before? Could he be a rebel spy?"

"He's not a spy, sir. I don't know his name but I've seen him and his ox team at Ripley and on the roads around here. He works for Dr. Ellis on his plantation."

"Where's that, Randall?"

"About four miles this side of Ripley, sir."

"How big a plantation is it?"

"Couple hundred acres, I guess. Dr. Ellis has about twenty slaves. Raises cotton and hogs mostly. Ellis Smoked Hams have a reputation from here to Vicksburg, sir."

Colonel Grierson smiled. "Smoked ham? Ah! You know, I think we might manage to bivouac there tonight. You and Marksbury ride in the advance guard. Be careful of ambush."

Baxie and Marksbury both saluted. "Yes, sir," they said.

At the end of the regulation thirty-mile cavalry march the vanguard of the Seventh Illinois was at the northern fences of Dr. Ellis's plantation. Scrawny corn barely peeped through the dry, caked fields; the plantation looked uncared for.

Soon afterward they came into view of the white pillared mansion and the barns and other outbuildings. All were in need of paint and all seemed deserted. Baxie had passed the place many times before and it had always been bustling with the activities of slaves. Now there was only silence and the great white house standing empty and staring.

Baxie saw something else, a flicker of white moving away from one of the smokehouses behind the mansion. He yelled, "Pegasus!"

He kicked Belle in the ribs and galloped down the road toward the gate. Marksbury and a dozen troopers galloped after him. They hadn't seen anything but the excitement seemed to have rubbed off on them. "Where are you going?" Marksbury yelled.

"There! Back of the smokehouse! Colonel Dark and some of his men! He's riding Pegasus!"

Dark and his riders, who had evidently been interrupted while pillaging some supplies, were now aware of the Union riders. They tossed double sacks across the horns of their saddles and spurred away across the fields. They were racing for the shelter of some short-leaf pines.

"If they make the timber they'll get away!" Baxie yelled.

The troopers were fast overhauling the last three of Dark's riders but the white Pegasus was a blur of speed. He fairly flew over the ground toward the timber. He was far in advance now and widening his advantage at every stride. He vanished into the cover of the pines. Two of the riders behind him made it safely, too. The three riders in the rear did not.

Baxie shouted, "Halt, Johnny Rebs, or we shoot!"

Three dirty, unkempt men on dirty, unkempt mounts pulled up and stared sullenly at their captors. They dropped twin sacks off the horns of their saddles, which plopped heavily into the dirt. One of the Union riders grinned at his mates. "I can smell that there ham through them sacks."

One of Dark's men said, with a surly scowl, "We were just hungry, Billy Yank, that's all."

Baxie said, "These men aren't Rebels, Dan. They're guerillas. The man on the white horse was Colonel Dark. He killed my father. I'm going after him." He kicked Belle in the ribs and the horse leaped away.

Marksbury spurred after him and grabbed Belle's reins. He pulled the roan to a stop. "You're going to obey orders, boy! You're in the cavalry now. You can't go traipsing over the country just because you got yourself a notion to catch a white horse."

"Pegasus belongs to me. Dad told me to get him back. The last thing Dad said was . . ."

Marksbury said, "I know how you feel, boy. But you can't go off chasing Colonel Dark. Colonel Grierson told me to look after you. In this man's army, boy, deserters get themselves shot!"

6.

Battle at the Bridge

BAXIE RANDALL was curled up in his blanket with his feet to a dead fire. He had slept fitfully most of the night, unconsciously living over the tragedy of the day before. But near morning he fell into a deep sleep.

He awakened with a start when an unfamiliar sound blasted through the air. He raised his body and tossed back the blanket. His eyes stared into the darkness. He located the sound at last . . . a bugler etched against the backdrop of the sky.

Then he heard Marksbury's merry laugh. "Didn't you ever hear a bugle call before, Baxie? That's reveille. It means get up. Now."

Baxie yawned and put his body down and pulled

the blanket back over him. "The stars are still out, Corporal. No use getting up yet."

He felt Marksbury's boot playfully prod into his ribs. Marksbury said, "On your feet, soldier! That bugler is not playing a solo. That reveille is an order! Get out of that blanket!"

Baxie rolled over and sprang to his feet at the urgency in Marksbury's voice. He saluted and said, "Yes, sir. I'm sorry, sir."

"Roll your blanket inside your poncho. Feed your horse. Help Simmons with the squad fire."

"Yes, sir." Baxie moved away from the dead fire and found his mare. He almost bumped into Simmons in the darkness, returning from the creek with a pail of water. They built a fire and made coffee and broke out hardtack. They fried slabs of Dr. Ellis's ham that they had commandeered from the smokehouses the night before. Soon the aroma of ham and coffee was drifting through the trees. The darkness got a rosy tint as the sun came up far beyond the trees to the east. Birds began to chirp.

Marksbury came back from a visit to the Captain's tent and alerted his men. "Those men we nabbed last night got the Captain plenty scared with their stories about the Rebels."

"Colonel Dark's guerillas can't be trusted. They're champion liars."

"What they said backs up what Dr. Ellis's slaves

told us. We're right smack dab in the middle of a hornet's nest of Rebels. In the first place, a Major Alexander has got his 18th Mississippi Cavalry camped near King's Bridge. Know where that is, Baxie?"

"A little west of here. If the Captain figures the Rebels are breathing down our necks, why does he have the bugler blow so loud? The Rebels could hear him clear over to the Mississippi River and down to the Yazoo."

"Bugle calls don't travel good in timber, boy. You can depend on it, Grierson wouldn't risk warning Colonel Barteau."

"Who's Barteau?"

"A ripsnorting whing-ding of a Rebel! Colonel Barteau heads the 2nd Tennessee Cavalry for the Rebs. The Rebs got more than a thousand men all around us in a twenty-mile circle. We're going to have our hands full to slip through."

"What about Colonel Dark and his guerillas?"

"They're busy stealing anything that's loose at both ends. They raid both sides. Yesterday they beat up an old man in the feed store in Ripley. Then they came to raid the smokehouses here."

"How about Pegasus?"

"That was your stallion Dark was riding, all right. But it looks like you'll never get a chance to get him back."

"Why not?"

"According to one of the men we captured, Colonel Dark is headed southwest toward Grenada. That's the wrong direction for us . . . we're headed straight south. I asked the captain."

A bugle pealed out its mellow song through the timber. Marksbury shouted, "Ready, men! We're pulling out."

Baxie said, "How do you know that? Nobody gave an order. The Captain hasn't shown his face yet."

"The bugle, boy. It gives orders for the Captain. You'll learn the bugle calls and get used to them. Many of them sound alike but they all mean something different."

They doused the fire then and did what Marksbury referred to jokingly as "police the camp." It simply meant that the men kicked the now dead fires apart and scattered the ashes with their boots. "That ain't the real name for it," Marksbury admitted, "but the idea is we don't want to make it too easy for some Johnny Reb to count our camp fires and figure out that there were more than a thousand Federal cavalrymen camped here last night."

Baxie chuckled as he led Belle to the stump of a tree so he could climb into her saddle without help. "I wouldn't need any camp fires to tell me there were horses here . . . and how many."

Marksbury grinned and did not take offense. "You

wouldn't, but how about the Rebs? I always did say we were smarter than them."

A bugle pealed. Marksbury leaped on his big black and kneed him over next to Baxie's roan. He looked behind him at the long line forming in the trees, two by two. Lieutenant Lancaster rode up, that eternal smile on his face. He didn't say anything. He pointed silently ahead.

Baxie grinned. "Ripley?"

Lancaster said, "You know where it is; lead us to it."

The long line of silent riders moved down the rutted road, saddles creaking, bits jingling, arms rattling, the hooves of the horses making queer *plops* of sound in the deep dust. As the troopers maintained their steady three-mile-an-hour cavalry pace an occasional mounted trooper would nudge his mount into line from the timber. These men had been serving as pickets during the night and now were falling in with their proper companies.

Colonel Prince's Seventh Illinois held the lead, with Captain Henry Forbes' B Company in the van, led by one of the youngest soldiers in the entire brigade. Behind the Seventh came Colonel Reuben Loomis' Sixth Illinois (Colonel Grierson was riding with him this morning) and Colonel Hatch's Second Iowa.

It was exactly eight o'clock in the morning when

69

Baxie led a mere handful of Blue riders down the little main street that was Ripley, Mississippi. Colonel Grierson did not want the inhabitants to be able to report to the Rebels how many Blue troopers were riding where Federals were not supposed to be.

Ripley was a collection of weatherbeaten houses with tiny lawns, plus a few stores that had wooden canopies over the board sidewalks. There was a small church with a square tower. Its bell had been removed but the bell rope still dangled there. The little houses had dog-trots through their centers and purple lilacs in the dooryards.

The inhabitants of the town seemed to be mostly women, along with a few men too old and some boys too young to fight. Baxie realized with a grin that he was only twelve years old himself and certainly not yet at the age to be a man of war. The people, most of whom he knew by sight if not by name, watched unsmilingly from doors and windows as the Blue riders moved cautiously down the middle of the street. Nobody gave a hint that he recognized him as the boy who just a day before had been living a few miles away as a neighbor.

In front of the livery stable Baxie leaped off Belle and ran into a wooden shed built in one corner of the feed lot.

Inside an old man was reading a Bible. His face was scarred and bruised. A bandage was rakishly wound round the top of his white head. He looked up from his Bible and stared at Baxie without smiling. "You're the Randall boy, ain't you? Didn't your dad teach you no better than to wear a uniform like that'n?"

Baxie told the old man about Colonel Dark's raid and the death of his father.

"Too bad, boy," the old man said.

"He beat you, too, didn't he?"

"He did. All 'cause I wouldn't give him no feed I didn't even have."

"We saw him at Dr. Ellis's plantation," Baxie said. "He was raiding the smokehouses there. We almost caught him, but he got away into the timber. He was riding Pegasus."

The old man grinned and winced when the expression gave him pain. "No wonder he came ridin' back here like the hounds of Hades was on his tail. I wondered what buzz saw he'd run into."

Baxie's excitement leaped within him. "Colonel Dark came back here?"

"He did. The white stallion was all lathered up. Looked like he'd been run all day."

"Which way did Colonel Dark ride? Toward Grenada?"

"No. Him and the men he had left . . . about a dozen . . . headed south down the road to New Albany. But they could be halfway to any place else by now. Wherever there's somethin' to steal, that's where you'll find Colonel Dark."

Baxie said, "Thanks, Mr. Galloway."

"Shucks," the old man said, "I wouldn't wish a rider like him off on any horse, not even a Yank's."

Baxie and the other members of the little force in Ripley did not know it at the time, but while they were in the village Colonel Grierson had called a council of war of his regimental leaders. He had a map spread out on a blanket under the trees and he pointed to it.

"The enemy thinks that we are aiming to cut the Mobile and Ohio Railroad somewhere between its northern depot here at this spot . . . Verona . . . and farther down . . . at Columbus. They'll probably suspect that Columbus is our target because of the military stores our spies know they've got there. Let's help them to think so. Colonel Hatch, you will take your command eastward in a feint toward Columbus and all the towns in between. We hope the enemy will be so busy chasing you and your troops they won't be suspecting that I've got twice as large a force cutting straight south. Good day, gentlemen."

So it was that Colonel Hatch and his troops rode east while Colonel Prince and his Seventh Illinois and Colonel Loomis and his Sixth Illinois started their steady march southward toward the little town of New Albany.

Baxie, riding scout with Marksbury, noticed that his thighs were beginning to ache from the constant rub of the saddle and the rocking motion of Belle. He groaned mockingly and said, "I'd give a lot to shuck my clothes and dunk myself in the Tallahatchie."

"The cricks you got down this way don't hold enough water to wet your whistle."

"The Tallahatchie isn't a creek. It's a river."

Marksbury reined up abruptly. "A river?"

"Sure." Baxie halted Belle. "What's so important about that?"

"If it's a river, Baxie, it might have a bridge. Or a ferry. If it's got either one, I'll bet you the Rebels got men and rifles guarding it. I don't want to go riding into any ambush with our eyes wide open." Marksbury held up his hand to halt the column of riders behind him. Lieutenant Lancaster soon came riding up. "What's up, Corporal?"

Marksbury told him. The Lieutenant then asked Baxie all he knew about the bridge and the river and the terrain on both sides of it. Then Lieutenant Lancaster called out: "Dillon, Vincent, Child, Alvey! Have your troops pull out of columns and follow me!"

Marksbury rode alongside Baxie. "Like I said, the Lieutenant figures the Rebs might be picketing that bridge. They might have a reception committee waitin' for us. Maybe we can turn the tables on them."

The Lieutenant kneed his horse in between Marksbury and Baxie. "You men stay handy." He waved at the little band of troops that had quietly formed into a tight little unit. "All right, men, let's ride!"

They drifted through the timber as quietly as possible, moving generally along the line of the road without travelling on it. Any Rebel picket would have a hard time trying to identify a double handful of riders moving like ghosts through trees where no Federal cavalrymen were supposed to be.

For about half a mile the Blue riders picked their way through the timber that skirted the road. Suddenly the trees petered out into a short stretch of hard clay dotted with tree stumps. The hardpan extended to the banks of a muddy little river spanned by a bridge of rough planking. Nothing moved in the area.

The Lieutenant held up his hand. The troops stopped. Baxie said, "Some Rebels are smart. They chopped down just enough trees so nobody could creep up on that bridge without being seen."

They sat quietly on their horses for a long time.

The Lieutenant finally whispered, "See anything, men?"

Marksbury said, "A bridge. Water running under it. The Tallahatchie, Baxie calls it."

"I've got a feeling there's Rebels on the other side."

"Why?"

Baxie pointed to a damp spot in the hardpan clay. "A couple of horses stood there less than an hour ago."

The Lieutenant said, "I figure if there are any there, they aren't figuring to get rushed. So, when I yell, we charge! Let's go, men. *Yeow! Yeow!*"

Baxie dug his heels into Belle's sides and the roan's hooves spurned the hardpan as if it were burning her feet. The Blue troops burst out of the woods. With Lieutenant Lancaster in the lead they rushed toward the bridge.

The wind whistled past Baxie's ears. Something tugged at his sleeve. He looked down at his arm. There was a jagged rip in the Blue cloth. Then he felt the sting and burn of the slug that had nicked him. He saw the white puffs of smoke out of the timber across the bridge and gray-clad Rebels running across the bridge planking toward them. He heard the angry *spa-a-a-t* of Rebel muskets and the whine of bullets tearing past him.

His blood was racing with excitement. His heart

was hammering. He was being shot at. Rebel bullets were whistling all around him.

The Lieutenant was screaming, "Charge!" He had his saber out and he was waving it wildly in the van. His men galloped behind him.

Baxie suddenly remembered he had a pistol. He had never fired a gun at a human being but he did it now. The weapon puffed smoke and the report was a crashing boom of sound.

Belle skittered sideways and stumbled. She went down sideways, her ears flopping back. Baxie let

go of the reins. He lifted his feet out of the stirrups. He was flying over Belle's head. He seemed to be going straight into the barrel of a Rebel rifle.

The world exploded in his brain. Then everything went black and silent as he crashed into the ground.

7.

Take Me Out and Cut My Throat!

FIRST Baxie's eyes popped open. Then he heard the blast of rifles and muskets, the shouting of men and the screaming whinnies of the horses. His hands burned where skin had been scraped off in his crazy fall but he still held his pistol. He became conscious of the smarting skin of his forearm. He shoved back the sleeve and saw where the skin had been scooped out and the thin scab of dried blood where the bullet had plowed.

Rebel pickets were posted at the far end of the bridge. Their muskets bloomed white puffs of smoke as they took pot shots at the Union horsemen. The Yanks had dashed past the north end of the bridge. They divided there and half swept down one side of

79

the bank and the other half galloped down the other direction. Then each rider dashed away from the river bank in a wide circle. When each had put at least a dozen yards between himself and his closest comrade they all wheeled their mounts and went dashing pell mell for the bridge again.

Baxie got to his knees with his pistol still clutched in his hand. Belle was standing nearby. That roguish white eye seemed to be winking at him. Baxie said with chagrin, "What a horse! The first time a gun goes off from your saddle, you nearly throw me into the middle of kingdom come!"

He crawled across the hardpan on his hands and knees to get to his mount. The Blue riders were blazing away at the Rebels again and the latter couldn't bother with one crawling Federal cavalryman.

He got to Belle, grabbed her reins, then led her to a tree stump. He hopped into her saddle. He joined the pell mell dash of his comrades for the bridge.

Some of the Rebels were trying to rip up the loose planking. Another Rebel was pouring oil on the wood and trying to set the bridge on fire. They had no time to do either. The Blue riders bore down on them, carbines blazing. Hooves hammered on the planks. Men shouted. Horses screamed. Baxie galloped and shouted and fired his pistol in the thrilling charge.

Then it was over. The Rebels had had enough.

They jumped on their mounts and galloped away from the bridge into the timber on the far side. Several quiet Gray bodies were left behind. A few others had waited too long to escape. The Northerners took four prisoners.

Flushed with the victory of the first skirmish, Lieutenant Lancaster gathered his men around him. "I'm proud of you boys, all of you. You'll do to ride with." He smiled at each of them and Baxie felt a warm thrill.

The Lieutenant went on, "Those Rebs were only pickets. There may be others nearby. We won't attempt to follow them . . . that's probably what they want us to do . . . follow them into an ambush. Instead, we'll wait here and get ready for their counterattack. Randall, you ride back and notify Captain Forbes! Marksbury, you set a detail to repairing the loose planking! Dillon, you post pickets on the road south! Move! All of you!"

Baxie said, "Yes, sir," saluted and spurred Belle back the way they had come. He delivered Lieutenant Lancaster's message to Captain Forbes. That officer notified Colonel Prince and the latter relayed the information to Colonel Loomis. The Seventh Illinois crossed the little bridge over the Tallahatchie immediately, expecting a counterattack by the Confederates.

The Sixth Illinois, however, with which Grierson

himself was riding at the time, never crossed the bridge. They crossed at a ford about three miles farther upstream.

While this had been going on, the diversionary force under Colonel Hatch, the Second Iowa, had ridden about four miles eastward in the direction of the Mobile and Ohio Railroad. Near a little town called Molino, Hatch's force was discovered by some scouts of a Rebel force under Colonel J. F. Smith and the latter began to pester the Federals with hit-and-run attacks.

Smith, of course, did not know that Grierson himself and two other Federal regiments were farther west, riding south. This was exactly the distraction that Grierson had planned.

Unable to fight Colonel Hatch with the small force under him, the Rebel commander quickly sent a warning back to Confederate headquarters at a little town called Chesterville that a Union regiment was invading Mississippi. He had no idea how strong a force Hatch commanded.

Colonel Hatch was also at a loss, since he, in turn, didn't know the size of Colonel Smith's forces. So he rode slowly and cautiously, so slowly and cautiously that he moved only about five miles below Molino during the afternoon. Every step of the way he was harassed by the Rebels who were not strong enough to offer him real battle but could still be a very effective nuisance.

Back near the Tallahatchie bridge the Federal troops could wait no longer for Colonel Hatch to rejoin them. The first rule of a cavalry raid in enemy country is never to stay too long in one place, never to let the enemy be certain where you are or where you are headed.

Colonel Prince and Colonel Loomis were ordered by Grierson to ride south. He hoped that Colonel Hatch might again catch up with them before night.

Grierson, of course, did not know if Colonel Hatch would ever rejoin them. Hatch might have ridden directly into a trap. His troops might have been wiped out in an ambush. Grierson well knew that he might have lost Hatch, and with him, one-third of his command.

They left the Tallahatchie and rode down toward New Albany. This was a small town nestled in a triangle of dusty roads that came out of the timber. The houses were small and weatherbeaten and seemed to be clustered together like eggs in a nest. Scrimpy curtains hung at windows, which were open to the April breeze. The streets were empty but curtains sometimes were pulled back to allow a housewife or an old man to view the progress of the Blue riders through the town. A few old men on the boardwalk in front of a general store watched them with no outward display of emotion.

The cavalrymen tried to buy candy and tobacco but there was none for sale. Baxie asked about Colonel Dark and Pegasus. He was disappointed when no one he talked to remembered meeting the guerilla or seeing the big white horse.

Baxie realized that Colonel Dark, after leaving Ripley, might well have ridden straight westward toward Holly Springs or southeastward toward Verona. If Dark had taken the latter road perhaps some of the Yankee riders with Colonel Hatch would have news of Pegasus when they rejoined Grierson's brigade, if they ever did.

Baxie told Marksbury, "These people are so secretive. Why don't they tell me about Pegasus? A horse like that can't come through a town like this without being noticed. They are lying . . . they . . ."

Marksbury grinned. "You ain't mad at anybody . . . remember. These folks are all nice folks . . . only half an hour ago they was trying to ventilate your hide with lead. Remember?"

"That doesn't mean they don't have a right to fight for what they think is right . . . or we to protect what we think are our rights."

By late afternoon Grierson decided he could no longer wait at New Albany like a "sitting duck," as Marksbury phrased it. However, when they did take the road again they moved at a slower pace, hoping that Colonel Hatch might still be able to catch up with the main force. No word came from the commander of the Second Iowa. No scouts sent eastward by Grierson could make contact with him. Colonel Hatch and his command seemed to have vanished from the face of Mississippi.

To make matters worse, as they moved southward toward a little town with the improbable name of Pontotoc, two days of good cavalry weather came to an end. The sun vanished, the sky grew overcast and shivery streaks of lightning outlined thunderheads farther to the east. Five miles below New Albany they decided to halt for the night on the plantation of a man named Sloan.

As darkness fell, thunder began to rumble. Spring lightning zigzagged across the sky. The air was humid. The troopers unsaddled, fed, and picketed their mounts in an electric atmosphere that made their fingers tingle when they touched the metal on bits or stirrups.

Some of the troopers prepared beds by heaping leaves or straw in a fence corner and then flattened it down with their bodies like dogs. Some hunted outbuildings and slept stacked up like piles of cordwood. Some crawled into blankets and slept with their eyes to the sky, hoping the clouds would not open up and drown them before morning came.

Baxie and Marksbury erected a shelter for themselves by spreading their ponchos over a frame of fence rails. They gathered dry brush for a bed and planned to use their saddles for pillows. They had scarcely prepared and eaten their supper of cold ham from Sloan's smokehouse, hardtack and coffee when the skies opened and the pelting rain killed their campfire.

Baxie and Marksbury crawled under their makeshift shelter, happy to escape the driving rain. Unfortunately, the wind rose and drove the rain sideward under the ponchos, finally ripping it loose from the fence rails. Before they could rebuild the shelter they were drenched to the skin and shivering in the chill wind and rain.

At that moment, Quartermaster Sergeant Sandy MacDougall chose to back his quartermaster wagon up in the fence corner. He had loaded it with edibles from Sloan's cellars, and was happily chewing on a huge sandwich made of smoked turkey between slabs of rye bread with caraway seed, garnished with sweet pickles.

The boys took the hint. They unhitched MacDougall's team, put on their nosebags and took them into the shelter of the timber to picket them. They then fastened their own ponchos as well as the sergeant's along the lower edge of the wagon bed, attaching the other ends to the ground. Faced against the wind, the ponchos thus kept everything beneath the wagon snug and dry.

Sandy MacDougall, still eating, crawled under the cozy shelter of the wagon bed that the boys had prepared and gave a long sigh.

Baxie said, his mouth watering, "How about some of that food, Sergeant?"

The Scotsman laughed heartily. "Didn't I tell ye lads? Me memory is getting poorly. The Colonel himself told me he wants to see ye at the plantation house right away."

Baxie said, "You old faker, you! Why didn't you tell us that in the first place, before you duped us into caring for the horses and building a windbreak under your wagon?"

MacDougall chuckled 'way down deep. "Ye lads wouldn't have been near so friendly like with old Sandy, now, would ye?"

Baxie said, "Let's go, Dan. Maybe the Colonel will give us something to eat that's better than Sandy's got."

The two soldiers lost no time in reporting to Colonel Grierson at the Sloan house. The full-bearded commander, pacing up and down the exquisitely furnished and shining room, wanted to be told anything and everything about the countryside. "All I've got, men, is a copy of Colton's Map of Mississippi. This rain has played hob with any fast cavalry marches. We'll have to outwit the Rebels by making them think we are somewhere else."

"Chesterville, a little town, Colonel, is off to the east. It has only a few frame buildings. There aren't many trees in or around the town. The Rebels couldn't defend it without a lot of men. But Dad always said the Rebels were using it as a horse-gathering spot."

"What do you know about King's Bridge?"

"That's back northwest a little bit. There's a lot of timber around it. A few men could hold off a lot, if they picked the right spot to do it. That's where Major Chalmers and Captain Weatherall of the Rebels are supposed to be."

"Where's the next big plantation? South of here, I mean."

"That would be Weatherall's, sir. Near Pontotoc."

"Weatherall's? The Captain is a plantation owner, too?"

"I believe the plantation belongs to Captain Weatherall's brother, sir."

"Thanks, son. If you haven't eaten yet, tell the orderly to take you back to the kitchen. Mr. Sloan smoked some mighty fine turkey."

Baxie laughed out loud. Marksbury followed suit. "What's so funny?" asked the Colonel.

They told him how MacDougall had tricked them into caring for his horses and building a shelter. The

Colonel, familiar with the wily Scotchman, joined in the hearty laughter.

At that moment the door to the room blasted open. A tall, extremely thin man wearing fine pants and a brocaded coat came charging into the room. The Colonel's orderly followed him, grabbing at his coattails.

The Colonel said, "Mr. Sloan! What do you mean, sir? Breaking into my headquarters like this?"

The plantation owner was red in the face. His eyes were blazing. "Breaking into *your* house? You blasted Yankee, I'll . . .!"

"Calm yourself, Mr. Sloan."

"Calm myself? You've taken over my house. You've appropriated my food! You have taken my animals! You have freed my slaves! You might as well take me out and cut my throat! I have nothing left to live for! Take me out and cut my throat!"

Colonel Grierson turned away momentarily from the irate Sloan. His eyes had a twinkle in them and he gave Baxie a merry grin. Then he turned around. "Orderly," he said, sternly, "as Mr. Sloan insists on having his throat cut, and keeps demanding it, take him outside and cut his throat!" He winked at the orderly so Sloan could not see it.

"Yes, sir," the orderly said. He took a huge knife from his belt and grabbed Sloan by his fancy coat and put the edge of the knife against his throat.

"Come outside, mister, no use getting your pretty floors all messed up!"

At that moment, Mrs. Sloan, who had evidently been eavesdropping, came swishing into the room in her crinoline gown. "Colonel," she cried, "don't add murder to your other crimes!" Tears ran down her cheeks as she hurried to her husband's side.

Sloan's face had turned from apoplectic red to a ghastly white and he seemed ready to faint on his own parlor floor.

"But, madam," the Colonel said, straight-faced, "your husband begged us to cut his throat. Now you beg us not to."

"Colonel Grierson, sir," Sloan said, "I reckon I just now changed my mind."

The Colonel threw back his head and roared with laughter. He wiped his eyes with the knuckles of his hands to clear the tears of humor from them. Finally he said, "Turn him loose," to the orderly. To Sloan he said, "Mind your words in the future, sir. Somebody might take you seriously."

8.

Through to Pontotoc

WHEN Baxie Randall rolled out of his blankets under Sandy MacDougall's quartermaster wagon on Sunday morning, April 19, it was raining steadily. The leaden skies looked as if they held enough water for the rain to last forever. Baxie knew the roads would be fetlock deep on the horses. Cavalry would not move fast nor far. But he knew that if it handicapped the Union invaders it would also handicap the Rebel hunters.

Baxie said a prayer while he was still under the wagon. He also read a few verses from the little Bible that he kept in his shirt pocket. Then he and Marksbury broke out some hardtack and ate some ham. They could not make a fire because they could

91

find nothing dry enough to burn. They tended their mounts and then Marksbury put some evil-smelling ointment on the bullet nick in Baxie's arm.

The rain stopped. Baxie went down to a creek and took off his clothes and jumped into the chilly water. He got out and stood naked on the bank and covered himself with lather from a bar of yellow soap Dan had given him. He then jumped back into the creek and washed himself off and got out on the bank to dress. Marksbury, armed with a razor that seemed fully a foot long to Baxie, was attempting to shave. Without a mirror, he would take a swipe at the lathered reddish whiskers with the razor and then feel his face to see if he had removed them. He meticulously avoided touching the stiff red moustache.

Baxie said, "That thing looks like the tail on a hobby horse I had when I was little."

Marksbury grinned. "That wasn't very long ago, was it?"

Baxie sat down on the bank and was shoving his feet into his boots. "Why do you wear it? You'd look younger without it."

Marksbury continued shaving. "Without it I don't look human. Take a look at that upper lip of mine, boy. It's a full two inches from my nose to my upper lip. That's that English parentage, boy. Without a moustache my nose looks like an Indian jumping off a cliff." He grinned. "Besides," he said, "haven't you noticed that the officers in this man's army always wear hair."

"You're no officer."

"I'm noncommissioned, boy, but I'm an officer. This army couldn't run without corporals and sergeants."

A bugle sang out just then. They hurried away from the creek and set about getting ready for the trail. It was the Sabbath, but armies don't have days of rest. Neither do colonels. Grierson was planning as cleverly as he could to outwit the Rebels. He drew three detachments of riders from the Seventh Illinois and sent them feinting in three different directions.

He sent Captain Trafton of G Company back northward over the road they had just travelled from New Albany, hoping to fool the Rebels into thinking the Federals had penetrated as far south as they dared and were hurrying back to their base at La Grange.

He sent another detachment eastward to hunt for Colonel Hatch and, if the commander of the Second Iowa was found, to dash on toward Chesterville. There, they were to disband the herd of horses the Confederates were reportedly gathering.

Grierson sent another detachment northwestward toward King's Bridge with orders to rout units under Rebel Major Chalmers. They were then to feint north a mile or more as if they, too, were heading back home.

The hope was that the three different units, flying off like sparks from a wheel, would not only win their objectives, but confuse the Confederates and hide the fact that Grierson himself, with a much larger force, was striking deep into the heart of Confederate Mississippi.

Baxie and Marksbury had been called to the Colonel's headquarters again for information about the terrain and they were still there when the Colonel was dismissing his commanders: "I'm riding with my old regiment, the Sixth Illinois, and we're heading for Pontotoc. The diversion units are all from the Seventh Illinois. Therefore, the other six companies of the Seventh will remain here, mounts saddled, until the diversionary units return from their missions. Then, Colonel Prince, you will follow us south with your entire command. Good luck, gentlemen."

As the officers trooped out, the Colonel smiled at the two friends. "You and Marksbury will ride in the advance, Randall. You know the country around here better than anybody in my command."

The Sixth Illinois, therefore, with Randall and Marksbury among the advance scouts under Lieutenant Lancaster, led the way south. The hardpan clay and the thick dust were soon turned into a quagmire, churned like muddy butter by the hooves of hundreds of horses. Yellow water stood in pools. The trees shed showers each time a rider brushed a low-hanging branch. The horses plowed fetlock deep in mud and progress was slow. The overcast sky finally turned loose a miserable misty drizzle that soon permeated the spirits of men and animals. All were cold and wet and miserable.

Baxie and Dan shivered in their discomfort. The mud was not only gooey but slippery, and the horses frequently lost their footing, slithering down on their haunches. Once Belle looked back at her rider with that white-wink eye of hers as much as to say: This is no fit day for a horse to be out.

One rider was caught under his mount when the horse slipped, fell and then rolled over, fracturing the trooper's leg. Baxie and Dan helped while the column halted and the injured man was lifted into the ambulance wagon.

Back on the road, his muscles beginning to ache again from the constant rub of the saddle, his nerves jagged from the endless *plop* of the horses' hooves sucking out of the mud, Baxie turned to Marksbury out of sheer boredom. "Have you got a wife back home? Any children?"

Marksbury shook his head. "I've got a sister."

"Younger or older?"

"Younger. Nobody could be any older than I feel right this minute, boy. I feel as old as that old guy in the Bible. Methuselah."

"Is she pretty, Dan?"

Dan chuckled softly and his merriness came back. "She don't wear no moustache." His good humor died, then, and he said, "She's got a withered arm, boy. When she was born she had it. I guess maybe that's one reason I never married. I'm kind of her mother and father and everything. After Ma and Pa drowned in that boat I guess I just decided to take care of her." He moved to ease his punished muscles. "I send her all my pay."

He looked at the boy. "Remember your mother, boy? Was she pretty?"

"Oh, yes," Baxie said. "She was from Virginia and they had a great big plantation and lots of horses. They . . ."

"Virginia, eh? Did they have any slaves, boy?"

Baxie hesitated.

"Well?"

"No."

"How come, boy? Virginia seceded and ol' Jefferson Davis has got his capital there in Richmond town. How come your grandpa never had no slaves?"

"Dad said Grandpa just didn't believe in it, I guess."

Five minutes of every hour the plodding column

halted. Horses stood in the muddy road, heads hanging. Men stood in the mud, hands on reins, leaning against their mounts in utter weariness. During these respites conversation died and men and animals seemed content to just stand still and try to regain their strength.

Not until midafternoon when Colonel Hatch and the Second Iowa rejoined them did Colonel Grierson order a halt for feeding and watering the horses along a thick greensward near an old farmhouse.

Baxie could see no signs of life as the little band of scouts approached it. They entered the ramshackle building cautiously, finding nobody. Baxie found a keg of powder, several old revolvers and a few old muskets under some burlap sacks in a summer kitchen. One of the men said, "Standing orders say we are to burn any building in which we find guns or ammunition."

Baxie said, "Don't do it. That would be like telling the Rebs we're here. The Colonel wouldn't want that. He wants to confuse them, not help them."

The man said, "No kid that ain't dry behind the ears yet is goin' to give me orders." He struck a light and touched it to the flimsy curtains at the windows of the summer kitchen.

The flames caught. The dry and blistered paint on the sills began to peel and bubble from the heat and soon the flame began to eat at the wood. Smoke rolled up and the flames crackled. Soon the wall of the summer kitchen was a sheet of fire. Horses began to snort and stamp at the smell of their ancient enemy.

Colonel Prince, whose Seventh Illinois by now had completed its diversionary tactics and rejoined Grierson, rode up and broke into a tirade. "Boy," he screamed at Baxie, "don't you know better than to set a fire in this forest? We could be turned into charcoal by the fire; not to mention being massacred by the Rebels. Go to the rear!"

Corporal Marksbury saluted and said, "Colonel, sir, Randall didn't set the fire."

"Who did?"

"I don't rightly know."

The Colonel stared at Baxie. "Who set the fire?"

Baxie said, "This is only my third day with the army, sir."

"All right." He turned to the Corporal. "Organize a bucket detail and use water from that creek over there. See if we can't put the fire out before General Forrest comes galloping down on us with his cavalry!"

The bucket brigade went into action at once but it could accomplish nothing. The house went up in flames and the walls collapsed in the burning ruins. Nobody would tell Colonel Prince who had set the house on fire. He was irate and continued to storm at the men but there was nothing he could do to punish the guilty one.

The column finally began to move again and the man who had set the farmhouse on fire spurred his mount up close to Baxie's and said, softly, "I'm sorry I was so bullheaded. I shouldn't have put the torch to the place. It was mighty nice of you, boy, not to blab to the Colonel."

Baxie was a little embarrassed. "That's all right," he said.

Marksbury chimed in and grinned at the man. "This kid is a real soldier."

Baxie grinned at the trooper. "Don't believe all that. I couldn't rightly blab, soldier. I don't even know your name, do I?" The soldier rode away, chuckling softly.

By four o'clock that afternoon the slow-moving columns of Blue riders were half a mile from Pontotoc. The scouts in advance could see the chimney top of the new brick village hall in the center of the public square as well as the spire of the church.

Lieutenant Lancaster spurred his horse up to the advance scouts. "I've just had orders from Colonel Grierson himself. We make a dash for the town. Just to see what happens, how many men come out to fight, what we can expect in resistance. We won't show our whole strength till we find out theirs. Randall, you know the town! Ride with me!"

Baxie saluted and ranged his roan between Lancaster and Dan Marksbury at the head of the advance scouts. Lancaster looked back at the handful of men who had charged the bridge at the Tallahatchie with him. "Let's ride, men!" He put spurs to his mount.

Baxie kneed Belle. The roan looked back at him with that white-patch eye of hers and then leaped away down the road toward the town. They galloped through the mud, slopping it in the faces of the men riding behind them. They splashed through pools of yellow water and swinging branches doused them as they rode underneath.

Puffs of white smoke bloomed from the road ahead. Musket balls went, *chugg* in the trees along the route they galloped. A handful of Rebel militia in makeshift uniforms ran out of a grove of trees. They knelt in the mud of the road. They fired their guns and yelped the Rebel yell. It was a spine-tingling thing and made shivers run up and down Baxie's spine. A Blue rider a little to one side screamed with pain and veered in his saddle as a minie ball hit him and knocked his carbine from his hand.

The Union troops drove on, shouting and firing. The Rebels contested stubbornly for a few moments. Then they broke and ran, throwing away their muskets. All but one man. He stood stubbornly in the middle of the road, disdaining cover, loading and firing his old musket. The Blue cavalry bore down on him. His resistance was heroic, but useless. He died there in the road.

As Baxie galloped past the spot he saluted. "There was a brave one."

Marksbury said, "But foolish."

The advance party galloped into the town, which had a population of about three thousand. The village hall in the center of the square was all but deserted. A few children stood wide-eyed on the lawn around it, staring at the invaders, surprised that they were not sprouting horns.

When the full regiments entered, the troopers searched out guns, ammunition and salt and destroyed all of it. They searched some of the more pretentious residences, but found only Rebel women wrapping bandages. The women were highly critical of what they called "abominable Yankee conduct." Captain Weatherall's Rebel militia, poorly armed and poorly trained, had evidently vanished into the wild timber country and would be no further problem to Grierson's well disciplined cavalry.

The new brick village hall was searched but was not harmed. All elected officials were serving the "noble cause," according to the Rebel women who had taken over their jobs.

Behind the village hall in a grassy spot Baxie and Dan came upon a dead horse.

Baxie reined up and pointed excitedly.

Marksbury said, "So? A dead mare. Looks like she broke a leg and somebody put a bullet in her head. It happens all the time. This probably happened yesterday."

"That's Tarheels, Dan. One of *our* horses. Dad traded for her with a man from North Carolina. That's why he called her Tarheels. She was one of the horses stolen by Colonel Dark. He didn't ride to Grenada. He was here. No later than yesterday. With Pegasus!"

Dan Marksbury, unusually serious, said, "We can't worry about no Colonel Dark and no white horse. We'd better start worrying about our own hides! Every hour we've been riding farther away from La Grange. We're a good seventy miles into Reb territory now and we haven't even seen a railroad yet . . . let alone cut one." He took off his hat and scratched his head. "What *is* Colonel Grierson aimin' to do?"

9.

The Quinine Brigade

AT TWO O'CLOCK the next morning, in half-darkness, buglers blared reveille in the camp of Colonel Grierson's Blue Raiders, five miles south of Pontotoc on the banks of Chiwapa Creek. Baxie Randall heard the call and rolled out of his damp blankets, rubbing eyes that were heavy with sleep. He massaged the arm that was still stiff and sore from the Rebel's bullet. He nudged his older friend. "Up, Dan."

Marksbury grunted and rolled over. "Can't see my hand in front of my eyes."

Baxie laughed. "Not with your eyes closed, you can't. Wake up."

"We ain't riding no place at midnight, boy."

"It's two o'clock in the morning, Dan. Maybe

103

we're not riding. Maybe the Rebs have located us. Maybe . . ."

Marksbury rolled out of his blankets, immediately wide awake. A sergeant hurried by, his gaunt face grim in the light of a nearby fire. "On your feet, soldiers. Inspection in one half hour!"

Baxie looked at Marksbury. The Corporal stared at Randall. "Inspection? At two o'clock in the morning? Somebody's crazy."

They stumbled about in the grayness, still fighting sleep. They kicked a dying campfire awake and sought dry wood to add to the flames. Other soldiers were doing the same. In a few moments the grove was choked with low-hanging smoke from a hundred

campfires. Coffee boiling in pots and cans added its aroma to that of slabs of ham frying for the fortunate few who had saved some from their last day of plenty.

After a quick meal and saddling horses, rolling blankets, companies hastily lined up for morning reports. Then the orders echoed along the banks of Chiwapa Creek. "Prepare for inspection! Prepare for inspection!"

To the veterans it was almost as automatic as putting on their uniforms or carrying their carbines but to Baxie inspection was still a thrilling thing. To look down the uniformed formation, everything spic and span, everyone at soldierly attention, sent a tingle up his spine. Each trooper stood to the left of his mount, face to the front, chest on a line with the horse's mouth, reins held with the right hand six inches from the bit, nails down, body erect. That was just the way it read in the manual Marksbury had shown him.

Sergeants and corporals moved through the formations, reporting in whispers to their lieutenants. The sergeants and corporals ignored most of the carbines and small arms as they were held out, but here and there they ordered a trooper to fall out. These men then formed a little square of their own in the midst of each company.

Baxie whispered to Marksbury, "Something important's going on here. Here comes Colonel Grierson himself!"

It was true. The Commander, in person, was talking to the troopers who had been ordered to fall out of the formations. Grierson was very intent, his black beard giving him a rather ghostlike look in the gray dawn as he moved among his men.

Baxie said, softly, "He's picking a scouting detail."

Marksbury grunted. "Not with Jed Dunnegan and Tony Hoffman, he isn't. Jed's had chills and fever, the galloping ague, for two days. Tony is raw and bleeding from that rash he's got. Everybody they took out of B Company is sick or lame. To my mind the Colonel is pickin' himself a Quinine Brigade."

"Quinine Brigade? What's that?"

"The Colonel's weeding out the sick and the lame men and mounts. Then he'll send the whole kit and caboodle back to the camp in La Grange." He whistled very softly under his breath. "The Colonel's fixin' to ride someplace very light and very fast. He don't want to be bothered with nobody not in tiptop shape."

Marksbury was right, but he missed one point. Colonel Grierson put the command of the Quinine Brigade in the hands of Major Hiram Love and he told him: "Major, you will march in columns of four, back the way we have come. You will march through Pontotoc, making sure that the natives watch you heading north out of that place. As you go you will obliterate our tracks and all traces of us. We want to create the impression among the Rebels that this entire unit has returned to our base at La Grange. You will also send a single scout from Pontotoc toward Oxford with instructions to cut the telegraph wires there. I hope, Major, that your subterfuge will allow me to be fifty miles further south of here by nightfall. Goodbye, Major, and good luck."

It was still an hour before dawn when Major Love and nearly one hundred and seventy-five troops, plus a few Rebel prisoners and a string of captured horses and mules, rode in columns of four out of the encampment on Chiwapa Creek.

Baxie watched them go, with mixed feelings. "They've got seventy miles to ride to get back to camp. The odds are all against them."

Marksbury chuckled softly. "They're helping us, though. They're fooling the Rebels. If the Rebs spot the Quinine Brigade and start chasing them, they can't possibly be chasing us."

This day the Second Iowa, under Colonel Hatch, had been given the advance position but Lieutenant Lancaster and Baxie and Marksbury had been ordered to ride with it because of Baxie's knowledge of the country. As soon as the full columns of all three regiments were under way the order was passed to "Trot." During the rest of the morning, at regular intervals, the trot order was issued and the Blue Raiders' average was far more than the usual cavalry pace of thirty miles a day. Even the noon stop for watering the horses and catching a quick lunch at Sakatouchee Creek was cut short.

The conditions were not ideal for cavalry riders. The roads were heavy, the sky was lowering and as often as not mist was driving into the riders' faces or mud was splattering them from their horses' hooves.

When they reached the town of Houston a small force was sent into it to gallop about and shout a lot of orders and create a lot of confusion and then dash out of the town toward the east. While this small group, of which Baxie and Marksbury were a part, was creating the diversion, the balance of Colonel Grierson's brigade was quietly slipping southward around the town by another road. The inhabitants of Houston did not suspect that nearly fifteen hundred Yankee troops had penetrated more than one hundred miles behind their lines and were still headed south.

A few miles south of Houston the Blue Raiders joined the main road and the troopers jogged steadily southward. Men and mounts were wet, hungry and exhausted. Nevertheless, Colonel Grierson kept them in the saddle until twilight fell. They bivouacked on the plantation of Dr. Benjamin Kilgore, just outside of Clear Springs. They were twelve miles south of Houston and they had put more than forty miles under their horses' hooves since daylight.

Late that night Colonel Grierson, still attempting to confuse the Confederates as to the number and location of his forces, decided on another feinting mission. Lieutenant Lancaster reported to his scouts that Colonel Grierson had instructed Colonel Hatch and his Second Iowa as follows: "Proceed to the Mobile and Ohio Railroad in the vicinity of West Point and destroy the road and the telegraph wires; then move south, destroying the railroad and all public property as far south, if possible, as Macon; then cross the railroad, making a circuit northward; if advisable take Columbus and destroy all government works in that place and again strike the railroad south of Okalona, and, destroying it, return to La Grange by the most practicable route."

Baxie and Dan Marksbury, as usual, rode with the van under Lieutenant Lancaster as the Sixth and Seventh Illinois moved south on the road toward Starkville. Colonel Hatch and his Second Iowa waited until their comrades had disappeared and then set about erasing all the evidence of Colonel Grierson's passage south. They even went so far as to take a two-pounder gun and turn it around in the mud just off the road in four different places to give the impression to the Rebels that Grierson and his four two-pounders had stopped here and then dashed eastward toward West Point.

Baxie and Dan were never to hear a word from their comrades of the Second Iowa until the war had ended . . . they would be too occupied in trying to save their own skins to seek out news of them.

At four o'clock that afternoon the advance scouts led the sodden, exhausted column into Starkville. It was a tiny, depressing place. A single street split a double row of white shacks down the middle. There were a few stores and one dilapidated shed had a sign over the door which proclaimed it was the post office.

Few of the Starkville citizens had ever seen a Federal cavalryman before. They stared sullenly at the raiders in Blue, hatred of the Yanks in every glance. One ventured from the boardwalk in front of the general store loud enough so the raiders could hear him, "If I ever seen a comic opera army, this is it."

One of the Blue Raiders grinned. "This ain't no army, Mister. This is a circus parade. We got Jeff Davis ridin' in a cage a little farther back."

The Blue Raiders destroyed a few sacks of mail

in the little post office as well as some obsolete muskets hidden in the attic.

They rode south again, their horses plowing tiredly through the sticky mud. Creeks and streams were becoming more numerous and most were overflowing their banks. At one spot they floundered through a swamp more than a mile wide. Rain collected in the hat brims and occasionally cascaded down over already soggy uniforms. Some of the riders had ponchos but most did not and the latter suffered from saddle sores, riding in their wet clothes. Steam rose off the hides of the struggling mounts. They were forced to ford many streams with their carbines and short arms held high above their heads.

Five miles south of Starkville, near Talking Warrior Creek, a violent rainstorm struck. Colonel Grierson was forced to call a halt. Men and mounts huddled miserably together under low-hanging trees as the elments hammered at them.

His teeth chattering, Marksbury said, "There's enough water falling out of the sky to float an ark."

Baxie said, "Then let's pray it doesn't keep on for forty days and forty nights."

From a Negro who had begged to be allowed to come with them from Starkville, Colonel Grierson had learned of a Rebel tannery nearby that was turning out boots, shoes and saddles for the Confederate Army. He summoned Lieutenant Lancaster and Baxie and Marksbury and laid out his plans. "We can't ride further. We might as well hit this leather factory. Take what men you need, Lieutenant. Commandeer anything you think our troops can use. Put the torch to everything else."

Lieutenant Lancaster, Corporal Marksbury and Private Baxie Randall picked out a handful of troopers from the Seventh Illinois who escaped the early hours of a dreary bivouac by riding five miserable miles through rain-soaked and mosquito-infested brush to the throaty accompaniment of a chorus of bull frogs. Dan said, "They sound like they're big enough to put saddles on."

They slapped at the insects, grunted at their tired mounts, swam a bayou a mile wide and managed to steal up on the tannery and leather factory as quietly as Blue ghosts, who, by rights, should have been nearly two hundred miles north. The tannery was a tall and ugly wooden building. Several lanterns burned inside and shed weak light out into the rain.

Silently the men dismounted and Lancaster gave his orders. "Marksbury, take your squad over to the left. Shake two men loose to cover the back. The rest of you follow me. Short arms and sabers only. No shooting unless you have to."

A queer excitement filled Baxie. He drew his saber with his right hand and carried his pistol in his left. He stole with the others across the muddy earth that helped to muffle their footfalls. They moved toward a wide door that was closed now against the rain but was undoubtedly used for the entrance of supply wagons. A wagon, covered with low-backed canvas, stood near the door.

At that moment a man's voice inside the building yelled, "Who's there?"

Baxie raised his foot and kicked the door open. The Blue troopers swarmed into the room, guns ready. Baxie yelled, "Hands up! No nonsense!" He pointed his pistol.

Half a dozen workmen, who had been interrupted in packing a wooden crate with leather boots, held their hands high. They seemed in utter shock at the presence of the Union troopers. They stood silently while other Blue riders scoured the warehouse.

Lieutenant Lancaster smiled. "Quite a haul, boys. This would have kept the Rebs in leather for quite a spell." He moved his saber and gave directions. "Take these men outside. Jones, Willoughby! Put the torch to the place!" He pointed to a pile of refuse in the corner of the building. "Spill the lanterns over that . . . it ought to do the trick!"

One of the workmen said, "You can't burn the place. There's a wounded man upstairs."

Baxie Randall sprang up the steps to a sort of overhanging loft. He moved over the floor to a dirty pallet spread on the boards. A man in nondescript clothes lay there, moaning. He had a bloody bandage on his head and another circled his bare middle. Baxie called for help. Two other troopers helped him carry the wounded man downstairs and outside. They placed him in the supply wagon, and then pulled it away from the building.

Jones and Willoughby went through the building with lighted torches. The inside of the building was dry as tinder and was fine fuel for the flames that soon sprang tree-high and lighted up the slanting rain.

One of the workmen came up to Baxie. "The wounded man wants to talk to you."

Baxie climbed into the wagon, which had been placed so that the light of the fire entered the looped canvas, flooding the face of the wounded man. Baxie sucked in his breath.

The wounded man coughed a little and a wan smile creased his gaunt face. "Thanks for hauling me out of there, kid. I figured some day I'd die with my boots on but I didn't relish being barbecued."

The man seemed familiar to Baxie; all at once he realized that this was one of Colonel Dark's men, the one who had known the myth about Pegasus. The man said, weakly, "You know me now?"

Baxie nodded. "How were you wounded?"

The man grinned wryly. "We raided a horse herd

just outside Starkville. Seems like they were saving the nags for Colonel Barteau. A bullet creased my head and I fell out of the saddle. An eighty-year-old man stuck me in the belly with a pitchfork."

Baxie asked, "Where is Colonel Dark now?"

The wounded man moaned softly and Baxie could hear his teeth grinding. Then he coughed again. "Dark's riding with twenty head of horses to sell to the Rebs we just stole them from." He answered Baxie's unasked question. "Yeah, he's still riding the big white one you call Pegasus."

Baxie said, "I hope you get better, mister," and began to climb out of the wagon.

The man laughed with raw humor. "I hope I don't. If I do, they're going to hang me. They don't care much for horse thieves in these parts."

Baxie said, "I hope they don't." He stared at the man, who was coughing again. "Which way did Colonel Dark ride?"

The wounded man moaned again, as if pain was forcing him to protest with his voice. "Colonel Dark? He said he was riding to . . ." The man's head suddenly slumped to one side, his eyes closed and his breathing stopped.

10.

The Real Target

THE NEXT MORNING, dreary and dull, saw B Company of the Seventh Illinois sent southeastward toward Macon by Colonel Grierson to make the Confederates think *that* was the target they had been aiming for all the time. By now, Colonel Grierson reasoned, the Rebels knew that it was only the lame and the halt of the Quinine Brigade that was heading back to La Grange. They knew that Colonel Hatch's feint toward West Point and Columbus had been just that and that Hatch, too, was headed home. They knew by now that Federal troops had travelled south through Starkville; they undoubtedly knew by now of the burning of the tannery.

Where were the Yankees heading? To make the

117

Rebels *think* that it was the important rail center of Macon, Colonel Grierson sent Captain Henry Forbes and about thirty men of Company B eastward toward that town. Captain Forbes had orders to ride toward Macon, double north as if he had achieved his object; then turn around and gallop southward to rejoin Colonel Grierson.

It was a sad and somewhat sentimental parting for Baxie Randall. He had been a part of B Company since leaving La Grange. For five days he had eaten, slept, gossiped, ridden and fought with these men from many small towns in Illinois and they had come to be his friends. Now they were riding off on a dangerous mission from which they might never return alive, while Baxie and Dan were staying behind with Colonel Grierson's main body. The Colonel told them, "Without you lads we'd have to grope our way toward our target. You are serving as my eyes, boys, as well as my map."

Company B, with Captain Forbes heading the column on his big bay, rode off to the east. Because of the almost impossible roads to the south caused by six creeks out of banks, Colonel Grierson's force had to march westward on a little detour of the Whitefield road. Even by taking the bypass they marched for about six miles with their mounts belly deep in muddy water.

This was the morning of April 22. Baxie, young

and enthusiastic as he was, was feeling the drain of almost constant riding. His thighs were sore from the rub of the saddle, the inside of his ankles were chafed from the box of the stirrups. His nerves were jangled by the never-ending *loop-loop-loop* sound of the horses' hooves pulling out of the mud. Now the discomfort of wet clothes and soggy boots was added as the roan Belle floundered belly deep in the water. The gnarled old cypress trees, the oily black water, the croaking of frogs, the buzzing of insects

and the electric feeling of peril around them all added to his woes.

"We ride and ride and ride," he complained to Marksbury, "but we don't fight. We've cut some telegraph wires and torn up a few tracks and burned a tannery but we haven't seen enough live Confederates to count and I'm no nearer to finding Pegasus than I was five days ago."

Marksbury said, "*You* want to fight? I thought you weren't mad at anybody."

The boy looked at Dan, his face serious. "I've been thinking about some of the things I've heard Colonel Grierson say. He was right. If you disagree with the government . . . or the police . . . or the army . . . you can state your complaints . . . but you don't go off half-cocked and kill just because everybody doesn't agree with you."

"That makes sense, kid. For a while I thought you were more interested in finding that white horse of yours than lickin' the Rebs."

"I want both, I guess. I want Pegasus. The last thing Dad said was 'Find Pegasus.'"

"Too bad the man at the tannery died before he could tell you where Colonel Dark was headed."

"Do you think he could be headed for Macon? Colonel Grierson said Captain Forbes was supposed to make them think *he* was our main force. *Them* means there are Rebels in Macon or there wouldn't be any sense sending Captain Forbes in that direction to fool them. If there are Rebels in Macon then that would be the place for Colonel Dark to go to try to sell the horses. Just my luck we didn't get to ride with Captain Forbes."

"The Captain's supposed to join us again . . . if he can. Maybe he'll have news of Colonel Dark and Pegasus."

Marksbury chuckled. He was riding with one leg hooked over the saddle horn to keep it out of the water that was better than stirrup-deep. "Even that white horse of yours couldn't make no time in going like this. They can't travel no faster than we can."

Baxie said, "We can't travel at all, seems as though. Captain Smith had to take the ammunition for his two-pounder out of the caissons and load it in buggies to keep it dry. Who ever heard of an army going to war in buggies, Dan?"

The road, under water for miles, suddenly raised out of it on to higher ground. The horses blew and shook themselves mightily and the troops dismounted long enough to stretch their muscles and rub their cramped legs. It was at this moment, when there was no splash of mounts in water, or rattle of sabers, or any of the other sounds that herald the approach of armed troops, that the drum of horses' hooves sounded from the south.

Baxie listened and said, "One rider. Sounds like

he's in an all-fire hurry to get some place besides where he is."

Around a bend in the road galloped a young, gray-clad rider on a lathered horse. He wore a jaunty hat turned up on one side with a plume waving in it. Dispatch bags flapped from straps across his shoulders. When the young Rebel saw the Blue uniforms in the road ahead of him his eyes bugged large in amazement. He jerked on his reins. His mount's hooves plowed furrows in the road and the rider almost pitched over his head.

"Ho!" the Rebel shouted. He reined his mount around in the road. He put the spurs to his horse and galloped away.

Baxie had leaped to Belle's saddle and he was under way before the Rebel had turned his horse. Belle was in full stride before the Rebel got going. The roan was happy to run on a dry road instead of floundering belly deep in dirty water and she really took the bit. She ate up the distance between her rider and the fleeing dispatch bearer with every stride.

"Ho!" the Rebel soldier shouted again. He took off the plumed hat and belabored his mount's flanks.

"Hold it, Reb!" Baxie shouted. He jerked his pistol from its holster.

The Confederate screamed something back at

him but the words were lost in the hammer of hooves and the rush of wind past his ears. Now Belle was ten yards back of the fleeing rider and gaining fast. "Hold, Reb, or I'll shoot you in the back!"

The Rebel's horse lost its stride. It stumbled and went down. The young Rebel jerked his feet out of the stirrups. He went sailing through the air, landing on his belly in the road, sliding far ahead of his sprawled horse. The horse got up, unhurt, and went over to nuzzle its rider. The Rebel did not move.

Baxie reined up. He leaped off Belle, put his pistol in its holster and walked across to the fallen Confederate. He had had the wind knocked out of him. His hands were skinned and bleeding and he was dazed but otherwise unharmed. Baxie took the Rebel's pistol and sabre and then rolled him over, face up in the road. The Confederate's eyes opened. He regained his senses rapidly and his eyes focused on Baxie's Blue uniform.

By now Marksbury and Lieutenant Lancaster had ridden up. The Lieutenant sat his horse, grinning. "Corporal, dismount and get the dispatch bags. Looks like Randall caught himself a nice prisoner. Maybe we can take a lot of Rebel orders back to the Colonel to read."

Marksbury dismounted and got the dispatch bags and carried them to Lieutenant Lancaster. The latter made a motion at the Rebel. "Get up, soldier."

The soldier got to his feet, staring angrily at Lieutenant Lancaster. He spoke finally with a heavy drawl. "Yuh-all'd never have caught me, only my hoss was plumb tuckered."

Lieutenant Lancaster ripped open a dispatch bag with his sabre. He opened a letter by running his thumb under the flap. "By golly," he said, after he had read some of the message, "this one's written in French. We'll have to get Pierre Lesure to read it for the Colonel."

He opened the second dispatch bag in similar fashion. This time he pulled out a double handful of Confederate currency. "Men, we got ourselves a million dollars . . . more or less . . . but I don't rightly know if it's worth anything."

He stuffed the money back in the bag. "Corporal Marksbury! Randall! Walk the prisoner back to the main body. Be sure he tries no tricks."

The men saluted and carried out their order. Lieutenant Lancaster turned his mount and galloped back to show Colonel Grierson their prize.

Baxie and Dan had fully expected that once they got out of the water-swamped roads south of Starkville the going would be easier. Instead, the roads were in worse condition. Once Baxie and Dan saved a trooper whose horse had almost disappeared in a mire-hole next to a gnarled old cypress tree. The water was black and oily and Baxie had a feeling that water moccasins and other snakes teemed in the swamp. He was glad when they finally got out of it and the troop rode silently into the little town of Louisville.

It was on high ground and the soldiers enjoyed riding on dry earth for a spell but the citizens of the community stared at them with cold hatred in their eyes. Many of the little houses and stores were boarded up. Somehow or other they had had news of the Yankees' coming and they fully expected to have the town sacked and burned.

Baxie heard Colonel Grierson issue an order to Major Graham. "You will stay here with your pickets until we have been gone an hour. Let nobody leave here with information as to the direction we have taken or our numbers. Drive out any citizens who try to mingle with our troops."

Grierson also gave a special order to Captain John Lynch. "Disguise yourself and Corporal Bullard as Rebel citizens and proceed eastward. See if you can find out if Captain Forbes reached the railroad. If possible, cut the telegraph lines. We don't want information about us flying down the wires to Jackson and other points."

Four miles south of the town the troops began a

long march through another swamp. Chuck holes four feet deep slowed their progress, but they kept doggedly on. Darkness fell early and the insects descended to plague the riders, already saddle-weary from a full day on the march.

At long last, after marching ten miles south of Louisville in almost utter blackness and under impossible conditions they reached dry ground around a place known as Bates Plantation.

Baxie and Dan almost tumbled from their mounts in sheer exhaustion. It was after midnight. With almost no rest for themselves or their horses they had covered fifty long and roundabout miles through swamps and morasses. At the same time they had eluded perhaps a half-dozen separate Confederate forces which knew Grierson was in Mississippi but could not find out where.

Dan, his face oafish with its reddish whiskers and caked mud and tired eyes, pointed off in the direction of a gurgling creek. "Before I crawl in, I'm going to take me a bath. I got mosquito bites big enough to put bandages on."

Baxie said, hardly able to keep his eyes open. "At midnight you want to take a bath?"

Dan chuckled. "If a Rebel bullet catches up with me tomorrow, I want to go to my Maker clean. And you'd better let me put more ointment on that bullet nick of yours."

Neither chore was ever done. They spread their blankets out under the branches of a hard maple tree and put their saddles nearby for a pillow. They tried the beds out to see if they were comfortable, and the bath and ointment were forgotten in exhausted slumber.

II.

Across the Pearl River

ON THE seventh day out from the Federal base at La Grange, Tennessee, the Blue Raiders finally were told where they were headed and what they were going to do.

They were going to do the impossible. They were going to cut the Vicksburg Railroad at Newton Station. They were going to smash the railroad that supplied men and materials to Confederate General John C. Pemberton at Vicksburg, where even now a Union general named U. S. Grant was assaulting the Rebel fortress that controlled the lower Mississippi River with all the power at his command.

If Grant could take Vicksburg the Confederacy

129

would be cut in two. If Grierson could smash the railroad at Newton Station, he could cut Pemberton's supply lines and make him an easier prey for the storming of his fortress by Federal troops under their bearded and fiery leader.

It seemed to Baxie Randall that no sooner had his head been pillowed on his saddle than he heard the rousing notes of the bugle the next morning. He rolled out of his blankets at once, his body stiff and sore from sleeping in the cramped position on the damp ground.

He trudged down to the swollen creek they had found last night and took off his clothes and indulged in an "all-over" bath. He put some of Dan's smelly ointment on the insides of his ankles where the stirrups had rubbed his skin raw. The bullet nick on his arm seemed safely scabbed over but he put some ointment on it.

Dan joined him then and doused his body in the creek, but this morning he was too tired to shave. Baxie put on fresh socks and squirmed into his dirty, mud-caked uniform and then forced his wet boots back on his feet. He washed his dirty socks in the creek and hung them on a bayonet stuck in the mud near a campfire to dry.

Realizing now that the chances of reaching their

goal and accomplishing their mission depended almost completely on the condition of the roads, he looked up at the heavens. The clouds were thin and the sun behind them produced a haze that made the sky appear pink instead of blue.

They put coffee on to boil and they scraped the black dried mud off their uniforms while they waited. Then they breakfasted on hardtack and some ham which Dan had wheedled from the dour Scot at the commissary wagon of Company B. When their food was washed down with the coffee, they fed and watered their mounts. Then Baxie got his dried socks off the bayonet and stuffed them into his knapsack.

He ground-tied Belle nearby and toted his blanket and saddle over. She whinnied and looked at him with that white-cocked eye as if to say, "When are we going to stop this stupid riding all over the countryside?"

Dan Marksbury was fastening the girth on Ebony. "Baxie, how far do you reckon it is to Newton Station?"

"Forty, fifty miles, probably. Why?"

"Think we'll ever make it?"

Baxie put the halter over Belle's head and she took the bit willingly. "Colonel Grierson has brought us this far. I think he can take us forty or fifty more miles."

"Every day . . . every hour . . . there's more Rebs headin' our way . . . like swarms of attacking birds. If Captain Forbes didn't make it to Macon and cut the telegraph wires south, we'll have the Rebs comin' at us from that direction, too. Pretty soon there'll be enough of them to gobble us up."

Baxie grinned. "I reckon Colonel Grierson won't let the Rebels gobble us up that easy."

"S'pose we get to Newton Station and cut the railroad and the telegraph wires to Vicksburg? What do we do then? Where do we go? The way I figure it, by then we'll be more than three hundred miles away from the base at La Grange. We'll never manage to make it back that far."

Baxie hesitated and looked seriously at the older man. "I hadn't thought of that, Dan. Where *do* we go after we strike Newton Station?"

"We can't go back the way we came. There'll be a dozen Rebs lurkin' behind every bush."

At that moment Lieutenant Lancaster rode up. "Mount up, soldiers! Colonel Grierson wants to see you."

They mounted and followed the Lieutenant back along the column to Colonel Grierson's tent. The Colonel was sipping a tin cup of steaming coffee while he pored over his copy of Colton's Map of Mississippi. He greeted the two and said, "Help yourself to the coffee."

He pointed to a spot on the map and asked Baxie, "I figure our position is about here. We've got one more obstacle to cross before we can ride into Newton Station. That's the Pearl River. With the general rains we've had and everything at flood stage it's almost certain it will be out of its banks. It's imperative that our troops cross it on a bridge. Where do we cross?"

Baxie studied the map for a few moments. Then he put his finger on a spot. "Right there, sir, or you won't cross at all. It is the only bridge across the Pearl for twenty miles. On the other roads there are only toll ferries. I reckon the Rebels will have all those ferries anchored on the south banks. They'll sink or burn them before they'd let you capture them and cross. Besides, it would take a week to cross a thousand men on those little toll ferries."

Colonel Grierson folded the map with an air of determination. "We'll cross at that bridge before the sun goes down." He saluted the Lieutenant. "Lieutenant Lancaster, take the van." He smiled at the three soldiers. "See what you can do about that bridge."

Lieutenant Lancaster saluted and that ever-present smile warmed his features. "Yes, sir!" He made a motion at Baxie and Dan. "Let's ride!"

The Blue Raiders were soon under way. The handful of picked scouts under Lieutenant Lancaster rode about two hundred yards in the van. Baxie knew that they would be entering the watershed of the Pearl by midmorning. By noon they should reach the Pearl River bridge.

"It's a high one," he told the Lieutenant. "They built it that way because the river goes out of its banks a lot. It's set on a trestlework, with guard rails running along both sides. If the Pearl is at flood, and I'm sure it will be, it's the only way a man can cross."

The scouts had been slogging along for several hours when a dispatch bearer came galloping up from the rear. He handed Lieutenant Lancaster a message and then saluted and galloped back the way he had come. The Lieutenant read the message and stowed it in his knapsack. Then he signalled a halt and moved his horse sideways in the road to face his handful of troopers.

"Men," he said, "we've been given a job to do. A dangerous job. Let's obey orders, stick together and we'll get it done. Colonel Grierson wants us to go forward on the double to the bridge, using extreme caution when we get near it. If the bridge is unguarded or lightly guarded, we take it. If it is heavily guarded, we send back the information and wait for orders and reinforcements."

He looked around the circle of grim and determined faces. "We'll move fast until we get close to the bridge. Then we'll move as silently as we can. We want no premature small arms fire. Is that understood?" He wheeled his horse, kicked her ribs, and the little group galloped down the road to the south.

They passed a crossroads where a tremendous slash pine, festooned with Spanish moss, stood guard almost as if it were a Rebel sentry. Baxie recognized the old landmark and kneed Belle over toward the Lieutenant's mount. "Lieutenant, if my memory's right, the bridge can't be more than half a mile away. There's a sharp bend in the road ahead, and then the bridge."

The Lieutenant raised his right hand and his little band reined in their horses. Belle started to whinny but Baxie leaned forward quickly and clamped his right hand over her nostrils. The Lieutenant said, very softly, "Divide evenly to both sides of the road, single file. Nobody in the middle of the road. Stay on grass as much as you can. No talking. Follow me."

The little troop divided and Baxie and Dan rode in the lead on the right side. They walked their mounts slowly, their hoofbeats noiseless on the wet turf of the road's shoulder. Now and then there was a tiny squeak of leather but that was all.

Suddenly a mule bolted around the bend ahead. On his back rode an old man who guided the animal with a rope halter. His skin was black but his hair was white and kinky. His face broke into a wide smile when he saw the Blue uniforms.

He kicked the mule forward and then sawed on the halter to stop the animal. He dropped the halter and dismounted slowly, his aged body almost creaking as he walked.

Now the stranger said, "Glory be! I heerd tell in Philadelphia last night as how Mistah Lincoln's sojers was comin' but I jest couldn't believe what my ears heerd." There were tears in his eyes and they ran down his grizzled cheeks.

Baxie said, "Mister, who's guardin' the bridge? How many men?"

"Half dozen. But they ain't men; they is boys from the town. They got themselves couple ole squirrel rifles and some ole muskets and they is playin' like sojers. But ah don' think none of them there guns'd th'ow a ball more'n thirty yards."

"You'd be just as dead if one of them hit you," Dan chuckled.

The old Negro said, "Their guns ain't dangerous. But they done took the planks outa the center of the bridge and they got themselves what they call com . . . com . . . combustibles . . . and they plan to set fire to the bridge the minute they see a Yankee uniform."

Lieutenant Lancaster said, smiling at the old man,

"Get that old mule off the road. Put her in the trees there. You wait till our main column comes up. Report to the first officer you see."

The old man nodded his head and led the mule off the road into the shelter of a copse of lilacs, smiling happily and saying "glory be" over and over.

Lieutenant Lancaster jerked his pistol from his holster. "Let's take the bridge, men!"

He put spurs to his mount. The horse leaped away down the road. Baxie and Dan and the rest of the little company followed him at full gallop. Baxie held a tight rein on Belle but she took the bit and sped across the hard-packed earth. He had his gun in his right hand now. They rounded the bend at full speed.

There stood the Pearl River bridge.

The river was out of its banks and muddy water swirled around the bridge trestle and lapped both sides of the road but the arch across it was high and dry. Rebels stood at the bridge, old muskets at the ready. They were young lads, in butternut clothes. On top the arch of the bridge Baxie could see the pile of broad planks that had been pulled from the roadway and heaps of brush nearby, ready to be fired. He could also see that the bridge was the only way across the wild and muddy waters of the Pearl.

One of the Rebel lads shouted, "Stop, or we'll shoot!"

Baxie yelled in derision, "Go ahead and shoot!"

The young Rebel pulled the trigger in his excitement and the gun discharged harmlessly in the air. He dropped it on the planks and it slid off and fell into the river. The young lad forgot all about it and dashed across the bridge to safety on the other side. The other young Rebels dropped their ancient weapons and fled, forgetting to fire the "combustibles" atop the bridge.

Baxie galloped Belle on to the bridge. He fired his pistol at the fleeing Rebels on the other side. He did not want to hit any of them but he thought it a good idea to keep them running. He dismounted where the planks had been removed and trash mixed with oil had been readied. He kicked the combustibles through the opening where the planks had been and watched them drop harmlessly into the river.

By now the balance of the scouts were on the bridge. Baxie shouted, "Give me a hand! Help me put the loose planks back!"

Willing hands helped and in a few minutes Lieutenant Lancaster sent back a messenger to Colonel Grierson: *The Pearl River Bridge is ours. Come forward on the double.*

Now the scouts remounted and cautiously advanced beyond the bridge. Baxie and Dan walked their mounts on the edge of the road. They were alert to their danger. The Rebel pickets they had chased from the bridge might now be waiting in the woods, eager to pick off the Blue raiders, one by one.

They came to a farmhouse, set back from the road. Shutters had been closed and as Baxie rode past he saw an old man riding off across a field. They passed other farms and they also seemed to be deserted. The Rebel pickets had spread the alarm as they fled and the farmers had all locked up and run. They would probably even now be in the little town of Philadelphia, eager to do battle with the invading Blue Raiders.

Lieutenant Lancaster raised his hand and shouted, "Halt!" He pointed down the road to the outskirts of the little town. He smiled grimly. "A welcoming committee," he said.

Across the road a solid line of Philadelphia citizens and area farmers had pulled a farm wagon and overturned it. Behind it stood the Southern citizens, aiming down the barrels of dilapidated old muskets and rifles. They were not soldiers or militia. None of the men wore uniforms. Most were clad in the homemade butternut jeans so common to the area. They were plain citizens, eager to fight the Yankees who had the gall to invade their sacred homeland.

12.

Death of a Leader

LIEUTENANT LANCASTER faced his men. "We will advance slowly. We will get as close as we can . . . until they fire. Their first shot will be our signal to charge!"

The band of scouts moved slowly down the road. Half were on one side, half on the other, single file. Baxie and Dan were on the right side. Baxie's body was wet with the sweat of excitement. His heart seemed to be making an awful racket inside his chest. He wondered if Dan was as excited and nervous. "Dan, are you scared?"

"My nerves are playin' tag all over my backbone right this minute," Dan admitted. "I'm so scared my moustache is even tremblin'." He laughed softly and it seemed to ease the tension.

Spaaaaang! A Rebel bullet sang its way toward them. A moment later they saw the puff of smoke. Another bullet kicked up dust at Baxie's feet.

Baxie dug his heels into Belle's ribs. He drew his pistol and charged down the road toward the wagon. He pulled the trigger. The explosion nearly jerked the weapon from his hand. This time Belle did not stumble. He heard Dan galloping along at his side, his weapon booming. He sensed the other Blue troopers galloping behind them.

The Raiders' horses bore down on the Rebel wagon. The men yelled wildly and fired point-blank. They were a few scant yards away from the road block. It seemed as if they were charging into a sheet of flame as they drove down on the firing Rebels.

Few men can withstand a charge of armed horsemen. These Rebels were not soldiers; they were only plain, ordinary citizens without any kind of military training. They threw down their arms in panic. They broke and fled toward the little town of Philadelphia.

The Blue riders gave the Rebels no time whatever to regroup. They stormed into the main street, and took ten men prisoners, commandeered a dozen horses and destroyed several stands of muskets and a hundred bags of salt they found hidden in an attic above a livery stable owner's house.

Baxie finally asked, "Where's the Lieutenant?"

No one had seen Lieutenant Lancaster.

They found him back at the wagon road block, lying face down in the road. His horse stood by him, nuzzling his body. He had been shot through the forehead.

They buried him beside the road. They stabbed an old bayonet in the ground above his grave, and fastened a little card:

Lieutenant Lancaster
Company B 7th Ill. Cav.
April 23, 1863

In talking to the livery stable owner in the town, Baxie learned that the local citizens had really organized their group to go to the bridge and burn it. They had heard the previous night from the leader of a group of Rebel soldiers that Union cavalry was approaching the town. They had been on the way to the bridge when the Union scouts had come upon them in the road where they had thrown up the impromptu barricade.

Baxie said, "Why didn't the Rebel soldiers help them? What became of the soldiers?"

"They rode off south. They said they were heading for Newton Station with some horse replacements for the Confederate garrison there. The officer was a big fellow with a turkey feather in his hat. He rode a big white horse. Biggest horse I ever saw."

Baxie's heart pulsed wildly in his breast. He turned to Dan. "That man was Colonel Dark! The horse was Pegasus!"

Dan said, "Sure as shootin' I think you're right."

Baxie told the hostler, "That man with the turkey feather in his hat was no more a Confederate officer than I am. He calls himself Colonel Dark but he and his men are guerillas . . . horse thieves is a better word. The horses they had were all stolen. Which way did they go? When?"

"They got here yesterday, late. They ate a bite in the square and slept on their blankets a bit. They lit out south about midnight."

The main column of Federal troops had now entered Philadelphia and Colonel Grierson had given strict orders against looting. Only those things that would give aid and comfort to the enemy were to be taken from the citizens or destroyed. So, the little general store at the corner of the square, tended by a white-haired woman who was at least eighty, had a mighty fine run of business and sold out completely its stock of rock candy and licorice. The Blue Raiders had long been without sweets of any kind.

Dan Marksbury was upset because the old lady

144

had no taffy candy in her stock. "All of a sudden I got me a craving for some taffy. I remember when I was a kid on that farm back in Warren County, Illinois, we used to have what they called taffy pulls. The mothers would cook up a batch and then the youngsters would flour up their hands good and pull the stuff and then cut it up and wrap it in little squares of paper and then they'd sell it for the benefit of the missionary society or something."

Baxie suffered a little from nostalgia. "We had taffy pulls on long winter evenings, just me and Mom and Dad, we used to make popcorn balls and we'd dip apples in some caramel goo . . . then Mom died."

Baxie was impatient when the Blue Raiders made no move to evacuate Philadelphia quickly. He wanted to spur Belle and take off at a gallop for Newton Station. He told Dan as much as they rode at a slow pace out of the little town, in no apparent hurry to reach their objective.

"Shucks, Baxie," the latter said, "what could one feller do if he did catch up with Colonel Dark and his thieves? The odds would be high against just one man. You'll need help to get Pegasus, boy. You can't do it all by yourself."

Baxie knew Dan was right but the answer did not satisfy him. He said, angrily, "Don't call me boy. I'm nearly as big as you are."

Dan grinned and his elfish face lighted up with humor. "I know you are, kid."

Baxie stared at his friend, anger flaring inside him. His face was red and hot words sprang to his lips. Then he saw the merry grin on Dan's face and he heard Dan's soft chuckle, and he knew how silly his useless anger had been. He saw the humor of it and he laughed right along with his friend.

At that moment Dan shouted, "Here come two Rebs!"

Fifty yards ahead, racing toward them from the south, two riders in butternut clothes came at them, shouting crazily and waving their carbines.

Dan raised his own gun and yelled at Baxie, "I'll take the one on the right! You take the other one! Don't miss!"

One of the secessionist riders reined his horse up sharply. The animal plowed up the road with its forefeet and almost sat down on its haunches. The rider took off his hat and waved it. He tossed his carbine in the road. He held both hands high in the air. "Hold your fire, boys!" he screamed. "I'm Captain Lynch!"

Dan Marksbury said, lowering his gun, "Sure as shootin', it's the Captain. Those Secesh clothes fooled us all right, after seein' them in Blue all the time."

Baxie spurred Belle up the road to meet the rid-

146

ers. He smiled. "I'm sorry Captain Lynch. Corporal Bullard. We never expected to see you coming back from *that* direction. We thought you were supposed to cut the telegraph wires at Macon."

Captain Lynch smiled grimly. "We wanted to. We couldn't. We found out the Rebs have two regiments of cavalry, one of infantry and two pieces of artillery in the town. We also found out Captain Forbes was about two miles away on the other side and we couldn't get through to warn him that the Rebs know he's there. All we could do was come back here and we had to ride seventy-five miles around about to do it. The Rebels are thicker than fleas everywhere. We were mighty lucky to get through. Where's Colonel Grierson?"

Baxie pointed up the road to the north. "Riding with the Sixth Illinois. They say he and Lieutenant Colonel Blackburn are cooking up some tricks to work on the Rebs when we hit Newton Station."

Captain Lynch and Corporal Bullard vanished northward around a bend in the road. Baxie said, "If Rebels were following them, they'll know we have a whole column of troops. Seems to me like every Rebel south of the Mason-Dixon line is pouring in on us, like water into a funnel."

Dan said, "And us under the little end." He grinned. "It might be good news that Captain Forbes at least got close to Macon. At least he'll keep those two regiments of Rebel cavalry from getting on our trail, too."

Baxie answered sadly, "I doubt if we ever see the boys from Company B again. Captain Forbes and thirty or thirty-five men can't fight two regiments of Rebels."

About five o'clock that afternoon the advance scouts reached a sizeable plantation and sent back word to Colonel Grierson that it was well stocked with food for the troops and forage for the horses. Colonel Grierson immediately ordered a halt for three hours.

Baxie could see his chances of catching up with Colonel Dark and Pegasus slipping away minute by minute. "We're only twenty miles from Newton Station. We ought to get a bite to eat, feed and water the horses and then hit Newton Station. We could grab Colonel Dark and . . ."

Dan chewed on a piece of hardtack and smiled at his young friend. "You taking over the army, boy?"

"Well . . ." Baxie said, abashed.

"We've got twenty miles to ride. Right? That's four or five hours in the saddle. Maybe more, unless we do it on the double. By the time we'd reach Newton Station it'd be plumb dark and we'd risk ridin' our whole force into a trap. Instead, by waitin' here a few hours and then ridin' them twenty miles in the dark, we'll be just outside Newton Station

148

about dawn. We can surprise 'em, maybe, and at the same time be able to see what we're doin.' That's the way Colonel Grierson figures, I'll wager."

Baxie laughed. "Thank you, *sir*. I'll bet the Colonel talked things over with you before he made his plans."

Dan chuckled. "How'd you know that? The Colonel asks my advice all the time. He couldn't run this here army without it."

It was nearly ten o'clock that night when the final move toward Newton Station on the Vicksburg Railroad was begun. Colonel Grierson selected Lieutenant Colonel Blackburn to take the First Battalion and make a rapid march to their target. By midnight, the rest of the Blue Raiders would be following him southward toward Newton Station.

Lieutenant Colonel William Blackburn was a big, bearded man; so big that even his large-sized uniform stretched tight across his chest and shoulders. He was handsome, too, with ruddy cheeks. No matter how poor his fortunes or how dark the clouds he had the knack of always expecting something better ahead. He loved horses, was an excellent rider, and was fascinated by the dash and danger of cavalry life.

Now Lieutenant Colonel Blackburn sat his dun horse and stared up at the Mississippi sky as his four companies set about preparing for their dangerous journey. "Saddle up, boys, and fall in lively!" he commanded. He found time to speak to every enlisted man; a joke to the veterans who had fought often, a reassuring word or two to the youngsters who were still new to battle.

The evening had turned cool and the men shivered as they heaved blankets and saddles on mounts, doused campfires and stowed gear. Then the thin notes of a bugle put them on their mounts and they began their dangerous foray in the darkness to their final rendezvous with the Rebels guarding Newton Station.

By dawn the next morning, April 24, Baxie Randall and Dan Marksbury, in the van of Lieutenant Colonel Blackburn's raiding party, sat their horses in the middle of a road and stared at the outlying buildings of the little Mississippi town.

Baxie said, softly, "There's what we have ridden seven days and three hundred miles to destroy. There's the Vicksburg Railroad!" He smiled grimly. "Somewhere in there, too, might be my horse, Pegasus!"

13.

The Smashing of Newton Station

LIEUTENANT COLONEL Blackburn came up to the head of the column. He spurred his big dun horse up on a grassy hummock on the side of the road where Baxie and Dan sat their horses alongside Lieutenant Joe Tabor. Tabor was a solid, round-faced officer who had replaced Lieutenant Lancaster as head of the scouts.

Blackburn held the dun under tight rein to keep her from prancing in the crisp, bright morning. For a long time Blackburn stared down the road at the little town. Then he said, "All I can see is a single railroad track and some scattered buildings. I want to know exactly where the depot is . . . both passenger and freight. I want to know how many troops are there. See if you men can find out."

Lieutenant Tabor saluted. "Yes, sir." He made a silent sign to his men and they scattered through the woods like ghosts. Baxie and Dan stayed close together in the heavy underbrush, rank with weeds that were tall enough to hide them.

They rode a tiny circle to the west, until they came to a single line of track. They crossed and followed the edge of the roadbed into the very fringe of the town. They saw isolated spirals of smoke curling from a few houses. The town seemed ominously quiet.

Here they dismounted and hid their horses in the brush and crept ahead on foot.

The railroad depot was deserted and the little wooden building was locked. There was a dirty, fly-specked schedule tacked to the outside wall by the ticket window. It showed that a train was due at nine o'clock. The single track was joined by others beyond the depot. Baxie whispered, "That train schedule probably don't mean much . . . it was for peacetime. Now trains might come through almost any time. The next one could be loaded with troops that would blow us all to kingdom come."

"That's good thinking, boy."

A couple of hundred yards beyond the depot was a large brick building that looked like a mansion that had been converted to other purposes. A handful of men, some of them in nondescript Confederate uniforms, were wandering aimlessly back and forth in the grassy yard. There was an aroma of frying bacon wafting on the very slight breeze but they couldn't tell where it was coming from.

Baxie said, "Those men are soldiers, I think. None of them is armed. That building is a hospital, I'll bet, and they're recovering from wounds or fevers. We might be lucky. There might not be any regular troops stationed here."

Dan said, "There'll be some soldiers, as sure as shootin'. And guns. The Rebs wouldn't leave a place like this without a guard of some kind. There'll be a home guard . . . militia . . . or something."

Baxie grinned. "Not if we surprise them enough." He pointed to the cluster of buildings beyond the depot on the wide single street. "The general store. The bank. The veterinary. The livery. The big white one with the porch around it must be a hotel or a boarding house . . . or used to be. I think Dad and I ate there one time on our way down to New Orleans to deliver a horse to the Parrish Brothers plantation."

Away off in the eastern distance a derisive toot sounded. "A train," Baxie said. He laid down on the ground near the track and put his ear almost to the gravel of the roadbed. He got up grinning. "I think it's a freight. It's heavy-loaded."

Dan grinned. "Must be arms and ammunition for

the Rebels in Vicksburg. General Grant will love us if we blow it up. But we'd better get our news back to Lieutenant Colonel Blackburn or we won't be able to destroy it."

The two ran back the way they had come. They found their horses, mounted, and hurried back to the commander. Baxie blurted out their information.

Blackburn listened carefully. He turned to an aide. "Pass the word. Encircle the place." He looked at his watch. "At eight-thirty-six the bugler will sound the charge!"

The aide rode off to pass the orders.

The little group of riders waited on the hummock for the sound of the bugle. When it ripped the silence of the sleeping countryside they would gallop down the road toward Newton Station. Perhaps to glorious victory! Perhaps to death!

Somewhere in the little town the Blue bugler sang his song.

Colonel Blackburn took off his hat and hit his big dun over the rump. He yelled, "Charge!" The little group on the hummock galloped down and away toward the town.

Baxie's heart was pounding. He could never get used to galloping wildly toward death to himself or to his fellow men. But he rode pell mell after their dashing leader. The wind whistled past his ears. Belle's hooves hammered on the earth, scarcely seeming to touch the ground. Dan Marksbury yelled crazily beside him.

Blackburn's big dun led the way into the wide, single street of the town. A few startled citizens who had run into the street at the sound of the bugle were now running for cover. The uniformed men around the big building scurried inside, as if running for weapons. Blackburn yelled, "Smash the telegraph office!"

Baxie and Dan were closest. Baxie pulled Belle up sharply and her hooves plowed furrows in the dirt. He and Dan leaped off their mounts. They sprinted across the depot platform. Baxie knocked the glass out of the door and tried to work the latch. The wood was swelled shut and the door would not open. He drew back his foot and kicked the door off its hinges.

They ran into the small office. The telegraph instrument rested on a rough table by the window that looked out on the track. Baxie smashed it with one blow of his pistol butt. Dan gleefully ripped the wires from the table and from the wall.

They ran back outside. Blackburn was in his saddle in the middle of the street, astride the big dun, shouting orders. "Block all the roads into town! Make sure nobody escapes from any of the buildings!"

Baxie and Dan dismounted in front of the livery stable. The wide doorway led inside to deep shadows. An old man with a white beard came hobbling out of it into the street. He carried an old musket. He was shouting insanely, pointing the gun at the two Union troopers.

Baxie drew his revolver. "Drop it, old man, or I'll have to kill you!"

The old man stared at them balefully but he dropped the musket in the dust. "Get back inside!" Baxie ordered. He and Dan led their mounts inside, following the old man into the eerie dark of the building. They could hear the faint stirrings of horses in some of the stalls at the rear. They put their own mounts in stalls. Then they hurried back to stand just inside the doorway. Here, they could see everything that happened in the little town without being seen.

The Blue Raiders threw the switches on the main track so the oncoming train could not go on through but would automatically be shunted to the siding. While this was going on, Rebels who had attempted to get out into the street from various buildings were disarmed, tied up and stowed away inside the buildings.

Toot! Toot!

The comic opera sound of the old train engine almost made Baxie laugh, in spite of the seriousness of their mission. It approached through the pines, belching black smoke into the azure sky. The cowcatcher showed first around the bend, then the entire train. The wheels pounded on the rail joints, the locomotive puffed, the cars rattled and moaned as the train pulled up even with the depot.

The engineer, calmly puffing on a cheroot in his cab, brought it to a halt. A brakeman dropped off a side step to throw the switch so they could pull off on the siding to unload their cargo. He looked surprised when he found the switch already thrown and he looked more surprised when a Union cavalryman jumped out of the weeds and stuck a sabre in the middle of his back.

"Get back on that engine, Johnny Reb, and keep your mouth shut or I'll cut my initials in your gizzard!"

The brakeman scrambled back on the engine in a hurry.

The Blue Raiders came out of their hiding places. They came out of buildings and from the undergrowth along the tracks. They took over the train. Baxie and Dan were now in the forefront, excitement driving them.

The train was part passenger, part freight. Four cars were loaded with guns and ammunition destined for the Confederate forces of General John C. Pemberton at Vicksburg. He would never receive them now, and Union General U. S. Grant would thank his lucky stars that a man named Grierson who didn't even like horses had directed a cavalry foray that was absolutely brilliant in execution.

Newton Station was now a bedlam of dust, smoke, steam and confusion. What the First Battalion could not use of arms and ammunition was fired and blown up. Two other railroad cars loaded with quartermaster and commissary stores were drenched with oil and set aflame. The locomotive itself was backed up eastward a couple of hundred yards and blown up. While this was going on the artillery shells in the burning railroad cars began to explode.

Hearing all this racket from his post in the lead of the main column that had not yet reached Newton Station, Colonel Grierson assumed that Blackburn had run into a trap and was being shelled by Rebel artillery. He gave the order, "Forward! On the double!"

Soon a thousand Blue uniforms crowded the streets of the town.

Now overjoyed that Blackburn had performed his job so well, Grierson immediately set about making the destruction of Newton Station complete. He sent Major Matthew Starr of the Sixth Illinois to the east with orders to burn any bridges or trestleworks they found. They were also to cut down and destroy telegraph poles or make them unusable by the enemy. They were to destroy anything they found as far east as the Chunkey River, that could be of aid or comfort to the enemy. Captain Joseph Herring of Company K was given an assignment like Starr's, except that he was to work westward out of Newton Station.

The Blue Raiders who remained in the little town were also kept busy. They put the torch to a frame warehouse that had five hundred small arms and some Confederate uniforms hidden under the floors. With crowbars taken from the depot the Raiders tore up the railroad tracks and pried up the ties. They made huge bonfires and heated the rails until they became white hot, and the iron became so soft and malleable that the Raiders were literally able to tie knots in the rails by walking each end around a tree.

While all this was going on Adjutant George Root of the Seventh Illinois set up a table in the hospital and got seventy-five Confederate prisoners on the parole lists. This meant that the Rebels could not serve in the Confederate Army until Federal prisoners in like numbers had been freed. Then they set fire to the building.

By two o'clock in the afternoon the once proud little junction town was a dirty, smoking shambles. Clouds of dust and smoke billowed skyward. The stench of burning creosoted railroad ties made the eyeballs smart.

One thing Colonel Grierson and every single one

of his men knew. The Blue Raiders, down to the last man of them, were utterly exhausted.

Now that they had accomplished the impossible and stabbed three hundred miles into enemy territory, destroying a heartline of supply to the fortress at Vicksburg, where would they go?

East? The Rebels were there, at Enterprise, with two regiments of fresh troops and a couple of six-pounders. Grierson's wearied Raiders would be no match for them.

North? They were three hundred miles away from their base at La Grange; trying to return would be suicide. Even now Colonel Clark Barteau and his Second Tennessee Cavalry were galloping down toward them from the north. Barteau had his pride and he would want to trap Grierson and humiliate him as Grierson had duped him.

South? There were nearly three hundred miles of unknown territory filled with Rebel guns south of them before the Federal-held city of Baton Rouge could be reached.

West? There were Vicksburg and Confederate General John C. Pemberton and fifty thousand men. If Pemberton had been able to hold off the stubborn U. S. Grant from Vicksburg, surely he would gobble up a little force like that of Colonel Grierson and his Blue Raiders.

Baxie Randall shook his head. Which way would

160

they go? Only Colonel Grierson knew the answer to that question. They had completed a glorious foray into the enemy's heartland. They had struck the enemy a blow from which he would not recover for weeks. But now what? Was it to end in the anticlimax of inglorious capture?

14.

Where Is Pegasus?

AT TWO O'CLOCK that afternoon Colonel Grierson ordered the buglers to sound rally call. Baxie Randall and Dan Marksbury hurried to the livery stable where they had hidden their mounts. As they threaded their way down the street they saw their fellow troopers sitting in their saddles in the afternoon sun. Their eyelids drooped. Their faces sagged with tiredness and were grimed with grease and powder smoke and dirt. Their horses and their own bodies smelled of sweat and wood smoke and creosote. Many of the horses stood hip-shot in the street, nearly asleep standing up. Many of them had thrown shoes and gone lame. Baxie knew that many had travelled miles without one nosebag full of oats.

Baxie thought: *If the Rebels should strike us now, they'd make mincemeat out of the First Brigade!*

They reached the livery stable and turned inside into its cool dimness. The old man who had menaced them with the musket was nowhere to be seen. They got their horses, first in the line of stalls, and prepared to mount up.

Suddenly there was a ringing neigh from the darkness at the rear of the stable. Baxie heard hooves hammer in the tanbark and he looked back, alarmed; then he saw a streak of white looming down on him out of the shadows.

"Pegasus!" he cried.

The rider on Pegasus was Colonel Dark. He still wore the turkey feather in his hat. His sullen face shone with hatred as he bore down on the two soldiers.

Baxie yelled to Dan, "Look out, Dan!"

It was too late. Colonel Dark swung his saber. The blade hacked down on Dan's shoulder and sliced through cloth and flesh. Dan screamed and threw up his arm. He fell against the side of the stall. He slid down the boards and lay still, his face white.

Colonel Dark slashed at Baxie with the saber. Baxie ducked and fell flat to the ground. On the way down he twisted his body sideways and drew his pistol from its holster. Colonel Dark's fleeing form

164

was outlined against the light of the wide front door. Baxie pulled the trigger.

Colonel Dark seemed to roll in the saddle as the weapon roared. But he did not fall. He turned in the saddle to hurl an oath back at Baxie, but Pegasus's powerful drive carried him through the doorway. Colonel Dark's head smashed into the crosspiece above the door. He was tossed backward from the saddle. He was dead before he hit the ground. Pegasus galloped away, the empty stirrups flopping against his heaving sides.

Baxie got up and hurried to where Dan lay, moaning. He knelt down over his friend. Blood was flowing from the gash in Dan's shoulder and it sickened Baxie. He knew Dan was dangerously hurt. He put his hand on his friend's shoulder and said softly, "Dan."

Marksbury moaned with pain, but his lips moved and he said, "Kid, that was your horse! You've chased him three hundred miles. Don't let him get away from you now."

"You're hurt, Dan."

"Don't mind me. Get after your horse."

Baxie said, his eyes fearful at the sight of blood flowing from his friend's wound, "Dan, I'll have plenty of time for that. You're badly hurt."

Dan mumbled, "Dad burn it, kid, do as I say." He saw the crimson stain on Baxie's hand and knew it was his own blood. He swallowed hard and looked at Baxie and put up his right hand. "Whatever happens to me, kid, send anything that's left in my poke back to my sister. You'll find the address in my . . ." His head fell to one side and he fainted dead away.

Doctor Goodall came on the double with his black bag. He ripped the shoulder out of Dan's blouse and took one look at the wound. "That saber sliced some muscle and he lost some blood but he'll be all right as soon as I get him bandaged up."

Just then a detail came to take Colonel Dark's body away for burial. Others, searching the stable, found the livery hostler tied up in a stall and he told Baxie the story about Dark's being in the building.

The big Negro, Bertman, brought the ambulance wagon and Baxie stood with damp eyes as he watched them lift his friend tenderly into it. Dr. Goodall said, "You two have become bosom friends, eh, son?"

Baxie said, his voice trembling, "When that saber slashed him, it slashed me, too. Will he really be all right, Doctor?"

"Sure, he will, boy." The wagon drove away from the livery.

Lieutenant Joe Tabor rode up, his face grim. "I've been looking for you, Randall. Mount up."

Baxie said, his eyes brimming, "I can't leave Dan now. He might die."

"Mount up, Randall! This is war, and you're a soldier. We can't choose what we want to do. We obey orders."

"But . . ."

"No buts, Randall. Mount up. Now!"

Baxie mounted Belle and followed Lieutenant Tabor out of the livery. The entire personnel of the Blue Raiders was drawn up in the street. Lieutenant Tabor rode to the head of the column and continued beyond to the edge of town where the other advance scouts were waiting. They joined, and without any spoken orders, they fell in behind the Lieutenant and Baxie, their horses pointed southward toward Garlandville.

"Randall," the lieutenant asked, "how did you and Marksbury get jumped by Colonel Dark?"

"I got the explanation from the old man when we found him tied up in a stall. It seems that Colonel Dark was planning to pull his customary trick in a new town. Last night he and his men arrived together. His men camped at the edge of town but Colonel Dark put Pegasus up at the livery stable.

"His plan, as usual, was to wait until early morning. Then he'd mount Pegasus and take any other horses in the stable along with him and join his men. He would have pulled that same trick this morning . . . but our Blue Raiders showed up. So he had to stay hidden in the back of the stable. The first time

168

Dan and I went to the stable I guess we took it for granted that the other horses we heard belonged to our fellow troopers. Pegasus and Colonel Dark were in the back stall and we couldn't see them in the dark.

"The Colonel discovered that we were burning and searching out the buildings in town so he decided to try to escape with Pegasus and the other horses while the town was in turmoil. Then the old hostler butted in. Colonel Dark knocked him out and tied him up . . . and then Dan and I walked back into the stable."

Tabor smiled. "I hope Corporal Marksbury will be all right."

"Yes, sir." Baxie paused. "Lieutenant . . ."

"Yes."

"I keep wondering if my bullet killed Colonel Dark."

"Why didn't you ask the doctor?"

"I did. He said my bullet was in him but it didn't kill him. He said hitting his head on the crosspiece of the door is what killed him."

"The doctor sure ought to know."

Baxie uttered a long sigh. "I'm glad. It's a terrible feeling to think that you have killed one certain man. In a battle it's different, it . . ."

"I know how you feel, Randall. And I'm sorry about that horse of yours."

169

"Do you think somebody in one of the other companies might have picked him up?"

"I doubt it very much. I think that some of Dark's men, waiting in the woods for their leader, probably caught Pegasus."

Captain Forbes and the thirty-odd men of Company B who had been sent toward Macon to fool the Confederates into thinking that the Blue Raiders were really aiming eastward were now trying desperately to catch up with Grierson's main column. At dawn on Saturday they galloped into Newton Station. Of course, Grierson's raiders were already fifty miles south by that time, riding through the Piney Woods country.

Captain Forbes had no way of knowing that Colonel Grierson had ridden south. Forbes took it for granted that Grierson had turned eastward toward Alabama and would then turn north and try to travel north to the base at La Grange. Accordingly, Captain Forbes and his little band galloped to the east toward the little town of Enterprise.

This move caused the Rebel commander there, perturbed by countless rumors about Federal troops that nobody could pin down, to rush the following wire to General John C. Pemberton in Vicksburg: "Enemy rumored 1,500 strong near Enterprise."

While the Rebel commander in Enterprise was trying to locate Captain Forbes's "1,500 men," the Blue Raiders themselves were well on their way toward Baton Rouge and the safety of that Federal-held city on the Mississippi River. In both cases, the Rebels were chasing will-o'-the-wisps which always seemed to be somewhere else than where the Rebels thought they ought to be.

On Monday, April 27th, about noon, eleven days out of La Grange, Captain Forbes and his intrepid men finally caught up with Colonel Grierson's main columns. There was a joyous reunion for the "boys of Company B."

Baxie and Dan, who was now able to sit up and ride in the ambulance wagon with several other wounded men, welcomed their former comrades in arms, and listened in amazement as they recounted their almost unbelievable exploit. One of them, punctuating his story with gestures and drawing lines in the earth to serve as a map, told them:

"We were away from you boys five days and four nights; we marched three hundred miles in ten different counties of this here state of Mississippi. We captured and paroled forty prisoners . . . and we either confronted or evaded several thousand Rebel troops at Macon and Enterprise. We got through or around the county guards at six little towns; we had been twice fooled and once lost and in all the time we were gone we had but eighteen hours of sleep. We didn't do much eatin'. Mainly because you can't eat very well in a saddle things you ain't even got to eat and besides, most of the time we was chasin' somebody or they was chasin' us."

Baxie said, "Captain Forbes can sure be proud of you boys. Colonel Grierson, too."

"Considering," the soldier said, "that most of us are only a year and a half away from a plowtail, we did a pretty fair country job of actin' like horse soldiers. Give me another hunk of that ham, will you?"

The next five days were hectic, strength-sapping days of almost constant riding, dashing attacks, impulsive and daring and desperate subterfuges. Men and horses were exhausted and dust-caked ghosts flitting through forests, fording streams, stealing ferryboats, evading capture, destroying bridges, slashing at their pursuing enemies. One sunrise looked like the one before; each little town they passed through was a carbon copy of the one they had sacked ten miles rearward or the one that was around the next bend in the road.

Through all this Baxie's face grew gaunter, his flanks tight and lean-muscled, his glance direct and grim, but confident. He was still a boy in years but he was a man in deeds and he held up his end of

172

the amazing exploits of their beloved bearded commander, Colonel Benjamin Henry Grierson.

Baxie was there when Colonel Wirt Adams and his Confederate cavalry were busily setting up an ambush for Grierson at the very same time that the Union commander's forces were already galloping away in the opposite direction.

Baxie was part of the exploit when the Blue Raiders, surrounded by Confederate cavalry slashing in on them from all directions, nevertheless managed to wreck Vicksburg's southern source of supplies, the New Orleans and Jackson railroad tracks near Brookhaven.

Baxie was at the plantation six miles outside Baton Rouge where Colonel Grierson was trying to keep himself awake by playing the piano he found there, and he was there when Captain Godfrey of the Baton Rouge Cavalry of General Nathaniel Banks sent a courier back to that Mississippi River stronghold of the Union forces to announce to the startled inhabitants that a brigade of cavalry from General Grant's army had cut their way through the heart of the Rebel country and were then only five miles outside the city.

The *St. Louis Republican* newspaper reported that "the information seemed too astonishing for belief."

Baxie and Dan were there on the sixteenth day

after they had left La Grange and nine days after they had destroyed Newton Station when Colonel Grierson's exhausted and saddle-weary warriors rode into the safety of Baton Rouge. They had successfully completed one of the most fantastic cavalry raids in the history of warfare.

As the Union troops rode in triumph through the streets in an impromptu parade, they were greeted by flag waving, bands playing and the oft-repeated yell, "Hurrah for the lads from Illinois!"

It was an unusual parade. The men of Grierson's brigade were so tired and bearded, their uniforms so torn and mud-caked, that it was difficult to distinguish them from the Confederate prisoners they had taken.

Baxie rode in the ambulance wagon with Dan Marksbury and they forgot their tiredness and exhaustion somewhat as they moved through the cheering crowds. They forgot their tiredness, too, in the realization and pride that they were "Grierson's men."

"Sure as shootin'," Dan said, "it's hard to believe. We killed or wounded about one hundred of the enemy, captured and paroled about five hundred prisoners, destroyed between fifty and sixty miles of railroad tracks and telegraph lines, captured or destroyed more than 3,000 stands of arms, and captured nearly a thousand horses and mules. If you ask me, boy, that's a pretty good sixteen days' work."

"Don't call me boy." Baxie smiled at his friend with warmth in his glance.

Dan grinned. "All right, kid."

They both laughed.

15.

End of the Trail

ON MAY 5, 1863, after the two friends had rested with the Blue Raiders for three days in Baton Rouge, Baxie was fairly bubbling over with good humor as he reported to Dan, "Colonel Grierson is going to New Orleans on the steamboat and he's taking some cavalrymen along."

Dan, slightly grumpy because he still hadn't been allowed to fork a horse, said, "Them cavalrymen won't be us, and it don't put no pay in my pocket nohow."

"He's going to take Colonel Prince and Major Starr and Lieutenant Woodward." His eyes twinkled. "Plus a noncommissioned officer . . . and a private. He figures everybody in the command right down to the privates helped in wrecking New-ton Station."

"So what?" Dan still wasn't in a friendly mood.

"You're the noncommissioned officer! And I'm the private!"

Dan yelped, "Why didn't you say so in the first place, instead of talkin' all day?"

"Colonel Grierson said we were his eyes and ears on land and he wants to see how we can navigate a steamboat. Besides, I think the river ride will help heal your wound up good and cure your grouchiness."

Actually, Colonel Grierson's main interest was to let the paymaster in New Orleans know that he and his men had not received any pay for weeks and had no money to celebrate their victory properly. He also wanted new wheels for the "Little Woodruff" guns that were all but broken down after six hundred miles of rough-and-ready dashing about the enemy country.

Baxie and Dan stood by the rail as the paddle-wheeler slid quietly down the bosom of the Mississippi. It was the first time Baxie had ever been on the deck of a steamboat and he thoroughly enjoyed the sights and sounds of the trip.

"You can almost hear the river talking," Baxie said. "You can smell the magnolias and the irises. Look at those tremendous live oaks leading up to

the white plantation. See that cotton field. Tobacco.
Did you know they raise a kind of tobacco here in
Louisiana that grows nowhere else? I think they
call it perique. It's real dark and real strong."

Dan said, "Their tobacco ain't much stronger than
their coffee, kid. Ever drink any Louisiana coffee?
It's black as the inside of a tar barrel and strong as
Samson. And these folks down here drink it around
the clock."

A particularly pungent aroma floated out over the
river at that point where a tremendous pine forest
stretched away. Someone inland was "cooking tur-
pentine," which is made from the sap of the slash

179

pine. The aroma gave a sharp antiseptic smell to the great river.

"Reminds me of the pine tar and honey Mom used to mix up for me when I had a sore throat or a cold."

They went around another bend and a big sugar cane plantation swept away over the low, flat land to a white mansion that dominated a high, grassy knoll. Not too far away downstream they steamed past an immense plantation where rice was the main product. Besides all this they saw acres and acres of virgin timber, and the farther south they travelled they saw more and more of the huge live oak trees with their fancy draperies of Spanish moss.

Baxie saw it all and marveled, "Peace and quiet everywhere. No sign of war and men dying. This must be like the Paradise that the Good Book talks about."

When they reached New Orleans the wharves there were not quiet and peaceful. Everywhere was utter pandemonium. Huge bales of sacked grain crowded the stalls. Cotton bales piled high as houses were everywhere. Steamboats and ocean-going vessels were loading or unloading merchandise of all kinds, bales, crates, boxes and bags. Teams of two, four and sometimes even six horses or mules pulled loaded wagons across the bumpy cobblestones that paved the piers. Fishermen were everywhere and the vessels of the fishing fleet lined the wharves and the smell of fish permeated the air. Anchored in the harbor were dozens of naval vessels, heavy guns peeping through breeches in their rails. Stevedores were everywhere, tugging and pulling and hauling things, shouting at the top of their voices, singing ribald songs of the south.

The citizens of New Orleans, or rather the Union garrison at New Orleans, went wild in their welcome. They mobbed the carriages that took the heroes from the docks to rooms at the St. Charles Hotel. There the Forty-seventh Massachusetts Infantry Band serenaded them with martial tunes. Captain John Smith, who commanded the garrison, made a welcoming speech and Colonel Grierson acknowledged it with a few words.

Baxie and Dan, wide-eyed at the sight of the big city, took it all in. They were heroes, at least the garrison of New Orleans seemed to think so, and the two were naturally excited over all the hubbub.

Next day Colonel Grierson took them on a leisurely trip around the city. They visited the French quarter and the old battlefield where General Andy Jackson had whipped the British in 1812. They watched the fishing boats, ate some Creole cooking and visited some above-the-ground burial places in the older sections of the city. They saw a Spanish prison that dated back to Spanish days and they visited the old St. Louis Cathedral that stood in the heart of the section that the natives called Vieux Carré.

Colonel Grierson also found time to visit the paymaster and then they returned to the hotel. A committee waited on the Colonel to inform him that the citizens of New Orleans would visit him that evening for the purpose of presenting him with an appropriate gift for his heroic deeds. The Colonel modestly replied that the victory had been won by his "Illinois boys."

"I wonder what the gift will be?" Baxie asked.

"Let's wait and see, boy," answered Dan.

"Don't call me boy." Baxie grinned.

"All right, kid." Dan was once more in great good humor.

That night the two friends, with uniforms washed and pressed and buttons and boots polished, attended the grand reception at the hotel, along with all the men whom the newspapers insisted on calling the "heroes from the Illinois country." Flags flew everywhere. Flowers were piled in corners until their scent filled the night. Bands played and soldiers sang on the street corners outside. Ladies in crinolines and silks and satin smiled at the soldiers and gave them juleps and root beer.

When Colonel Grierson appeared on the scene,

resplendent in his dress uniform, the Forty-seventh Massachusetts Infantry Band struck up *The Battle Hymn of the Republic.* Everybody in the place clapped his hands and shouted and stomped and cheered. Two little girls advanced on the Colonel. Each one gave him a tiny flag with thirty-four stars, one for each state of the union, and a bouquet of magnolia blossoms.

Then came the presentation of the gift for which everyone had been waiting. The crowd parted in the middle. Through the opening in the mass of people, led by a groom, came a magnificent white horse. His corn silk mane was decorated with ribbons, his flowing tail held a brilliant red bow. The crowd cheered at the sight. The mayor made a flowery speech and presented the magnificent animal to Colonel Grierson.

But Baxie Randall had tears in his eyes.

Dan Marksbury said, "What's the matter, Baxie?"

"Dan," Baxie sobbed, "he's lost to me forever now. That's my Pegasus!"

The next morning, early, Baxie put on his clean uniform and shined his boots to a high finish with a soft cloth. Dan rolled over and said, "There's no parade today, boy. Put down that rag and come back to your bed."

"I'm going to see Colonel Grierson. I've got to get Pegasus back."

"You can't take a horse away from a big man like the Colonel. The way I heard it the citizens of New Orleans chipped in their money and bought the horse to give to him. They . . ."

"The man they bought it from had to be a thief . . . one of Colonel Dark's guerillas."

"You can't prove that. You're the only one in this man's army that really knows that the white horse is Pegasus."

"That's right. But I don't think the Colonel would want to keep a stolen horse."

"The Colonel doesn't know that horse is Pegasus. The Colonel doesn't know the horse the citizens gave him is stolen."

"I'll tell him, then. And I'll buy Pegasus back from him."

Dan chuckled softly. "With what? Some brass buttons?"

"Never mind," Baxie said. "I'll figure out something."

It was nearly noon before Baxie was admitted to Colonel Grierson's suite at the hotel. The Colonel was dressed in a long silk robe with a red sash around the middle and he had on red slippers. His dark beard and his dark hair made him seem like a terrifying figure to Baxie. But then the Colonel smiled warmly and stroked his beard and put out his hand and took Baxie's. "What can I do for you, Randall?"

Baxie blurted out, "The horse they gave you last night! He's Pegasus! He's a beautiful horse, but they had no right to give him to you! He was stolen by Colonel Dark when he murdered my father!" He told the Colonel the entire story in one excited, uninterrupted sweep of words.

"Well, well," the Colonel said, and he paced back and forth on the carpet. "This is a strange situation, Randall." Then he lowered his voice and spoke to the boy in a confidential tone. "Frankly, I haven't had much love for horses since I was a boy of ten. I had a pony and he kicked me in the face. Ripped my face open. Left bad scars. That's why I grew this confounded beard . . . to hide the scars."

Baxie didn't know what to say, so he remained silent.

The Colonel went on, "I can't accept a gift from the fine people of New Orleans and then proceed to give it away as if it were of no value to me. Can I, boy?"

"No, sir, I guess not, sir. But I could buy him back from you, sir."

The Colonel hid his smile with the back of his

hand. "The white horse is quite a horse, boy. What is your offer for him?"

"I'll trade you my horse Belle . . . and six month's pay to boot."

The Colonel laughed out loud and turned away to hide his humor from the sensitive boy. "Who is Belle?"

"The horse I ride, sir."

"You can't trade an Army mount in a private deal, Randall. Your horse Belle is the property of the Union army and you can't . . ."

"Not Belle, sir. I traded Lucy for her. Lucy was a mare . . . with foal." His face set stubbornly. "Either I own Belle, Colonel Grierson, sir, or the Army owes me for Lucy . . . and her foal."

The Colonel paced back and forth. He stopped in front of Baxie. "Your argument is downright logical, boy. The Army certainly owes you something for the mare and her foal." He paused for a long moment. "Also, Pegasus was presented to me as a sort of representative of the Union Army . . . not for any personal exploit. . . . I didn't blast Newton Station all by myself. So, maybe we can . . . what do you say? . . . swap horses."

Baxie's eyes shone. "Yes, sir."

"But," the Colonel explained, "you can't ride the horse . . . any more than I could. He's too white, too big, too conspicuous for a cavalry command. Anyone who rode him in battle would be the readiest target for a Rebel rifle. Besides, boy, Captain Forbes tells me you enlisted for three years. You can't just say goodbye to the Union army any time you feel like it, just because you happen to own a white horse."

Baxie hung his head. "I know that, sir. I don't want to quit the army. I want to help to preserve the Union. I love my country, sir."

Suddenly Colonel Grierson said, "You and your father knew a lot about horses, according to Captain Forbes. Did you ever hear of a Morgan mare called Betsy Ross?"

Baxie's eyes grew big in excitement. "Did I? She was by Constitution out of Battle Flag. She was sixteen hands, milk white, with one black foot. She was foaled right here in New Orleans, sir."

"Right. On the Parrish Brothers Plantation." The Colonel smiled. "Now. Seeing as you and I have the little matter of a war to win, maybe we'd better set about doing it. The owner of Betsy Ross is a friend of mine. I think I can persuade him to keep Pegasus for you until the war is over. I think I can also persuade him to sell Betsy Ross to us and you and I will be partners. We'll have a wonderful stallion and a wonderful mare. When the war is over maybe we'll have a colt or two to come back to. Is that all right with you, Randall?" The Colonel put out his hand with a warm smile and sealed the bargain with a handshake.

Baxie's eyes were brimming with happiness. "Yes, sir, Colonel," he said. "I've even got the name of their first colt picked out. Something you said, sir."

"Something I said?"

"Yes, sir. You said we had a war to win. That will be the name of Pegasus' first colt: *War to Win.*"